HANDSOME LAWMAN

Handsome Devils Book 3

LORI WILDE
LIZ ALVIN

EPIPHANY
ORCHARDS

"Trent Barrett, I insist you arrest Erin Weber immediately. The woman is a thief and belongs in jail," Delia Haverhill hollered, her arms crossed under her ample chest. "Arrest her right now."

Trent scratched his jaw and considered the middle-aged woman in front of him. Delia wasn't what you would call the sweetest person in Honey, Texas. Truth be told, she put the cur in curmudgeon.

But still, as chief of police of Honey, he couldn't simply ignore Delia's complaint. And the woman hadn't, to his knowledge, ever had anyone arrested before. There very well could be some truth in what she was saying. A least a little.

"Why don't you tell me what the problem is and who Erin Weber might be," he said in a calm, soft voice, hoping Delia might follow suit and stop hollering at the top of her lungs. "Then we can figure out what's the best course of action to take."

Unfortunately, Delia didn't lower her volume one bit. She leaned halfway across his desk and said, "I've already told you what action needs to be taken. Erin Weber needs to be arrested. Now get up from behind that desk and come with me. I'll show you who this woman is and what she did. You won't believe her nerve. I was nice enough to visit her store last Saturday with my grandson, and she rewards me by stealing my Pookie. And to make it worse, she's displaying Pookie right outside her store. The woman belongs in jail, I tell you." Trent thought he was up to date on all the street names for drugs, but he'd never heard of pookie. "What in the world is pookie?"

Delia wagged a finger at him. "Get out of your chair, and I'll show you."

Reluctantly, Trent stood. "I'll be happy to get one of my officers to help you, Delia. But I have a meeting with the mayor in about an hour."

Delia frowned. "Did I or did I not change your diapers when you were too young to know your feet from your hands?"

His secretary, Ann Seaver, had walked in midway through Delia's comment. She raised one eyebrow and looked precariously close to giggling.

Trent shook his head and sighed. "Delia, I sure do hope you're talking about when you used to babysit me decades ago. If you mean something else, then one of us is seriously warped."

Delia was obviously not amused. She looked at Trent like he was something stuck on the bottom of her shoes. "Of course I'm talking about when I babysat you.

And I would think that means you'll be happy to help me now."

She gave him a squinty-eyed look. "After all, I never let you cry yourself to sleep like some babysitters do. I rocked you to sleep and sang you pretty songs."

Ann made a spurting sound behind the hand she had across her mouth. Trent was certain she wasn't the only one who would be laughing today about what Delia had said. No doubt Ann would tell most of the officers, and by the end of the day, everyone would be quoting Delia Haverhill.

Dang it all.

"Come on, Delia. Show me what this pookie is." He circled his desk and stood next to the older woman. "I think you've already shared enough babysitting stories for one day."

Delia didn't even crack a smile. She simply nodded and headed toward the door. When they drew even with Ann, his secretary was still laughing.

"What in the world are you laughing about, young lady?" Delia asked her. "Seems to me I changed more than a few of your diapers, too."

Ann turned bright red, and Trent chuckled as he trailed after Delia. That was one major advantage of growing up in a small town. Sure, everyone knew embarrassing things about you. But hey, you knew embarrassing things about them as well.

"So, Delia, how long do you expect this to take?" he had to ask as they headed for the front door.

"It will take however long you need to read Erin Weber her Melissa rights."

The bright sunshine hit him once they were outside,

so Trent pulled his sunglasses out of his pocket and slipped them on. "Miranda."

"What?"

"Not Melissa. Miranda."

Delia waved one hand and started down the street. "Melissa. Miranda. What difference does it make? Just read her the rights and toss her in jail. Now come on."

Reluctantly, Trent followed. He sure didn't like being ordered around, but as the chief of police, he had to keep the people of Honey happy.

"Tell me, what is this pookie stuff you think some woman stole from you?" he asked once they were headed down Main Street.

"First off, it isn't pookie stuff. His name is Pookie. Pay attention, Trent."

He thought he had been, but reading smoke signals would be easier than understanding Delia Haverhill. "Sorry if I misunderstood."

"Second off, it isn't just some woman who stole my Pookie. It's Erin Weber, the woman who opened the pet shop over on Collier Street. Naturally, I suspected her as soon as Pookie disappeared."

By now, he and Delia had turned off Main Street and were halfway down Collier. Delia pointed to the front door of a store.

"There's Pookie. Big as life. On display for the whole town to see. Erin certainly has some nerve."

Trent looked where she was pointing and bit back a grin. Pookie was a plastic statue of a rabbit, the kind you might put in your garden or flowerbed. The statue was old and well-worn and couldn't be worth more than a couple of bucks.

But Delia was cooing and fussing over the blasted thing like it was real.

"Now go on inside and arrest her," Delia said.

Trent slipped off his sunglasses and glanced around. As he could have predicted, he and Delia were starting to draw a crowd. Honey didn't offer a lot of diversions, so anytime anything even moderately interesting happened, everyone rushed out to see what was going on. He better head on in and talk to this Erin Weber before he found himself knee-deep in nosy citizens.

"Arrest her, arrest her, arrest her," Delia said loudly. Then she folded her arms under her ample chest once more and took on the expression of one who believes herself incapable of error.

Damn, what a way to start the day.

With about as much enthusiasm as a ten-year-old boy stuck at a Girl Scout meeting, Trent shoved open the door of Precious Pets and walked inside.

He'd only made it a few steps when a woman yelled, "Freeze!"

Trent froze as instructed and started to go for his gun when a petite, brown-haired dynamo rushed at him from the back of the store.

"Don't move or you'll frighten Brutus," the woman said. "You almost stepped on him. He's right by your left foot." She tipped her head, her expression more than a little accusatory. "He just escaped from the bath. Didn't you see Brutus when you came in?"

Obviously not or he wouldn't have almost stepped on him. Trent glanced around and didn't immediately see anything. But after learning what Pookie was, Trent wasn't certain he wanted to know what a Brutus might be. Probably a big ol' ugly snake. Or maybe a tarantula.

But curiosity got to him, so he looked down anyway, then breathed a sigh of relief.

Brutus was a little bitty fluffball.

"What kind of animal is that?" he had to ask.

The woman frowned. "A puppy, of course. What in the world did you think he was?"

Trent studied the round, white ball of fur with two black specks for eyes. "He kinda looks like a dust bunny."

The woman moved forward and picked up the puppy off the floor. "A dust bunny. Sheesh. He's a sweetheart, aren't you, baby?"

Obviously knowing he was being praised, Brutus let out a series of yips and yaps. Trent would give the puppy credit—he had an impressive bark for something that looked like a ball of lint. No wonder the dog had a tough name like Brutus. He needed every advantage he could get.

"Is there something I can help you with?" the woman asked, still cradling the dog.

"I'm Trent Barrett, chief of police here in Honey." He extended his hand, which the woman shook in a firm, no-nonsense handshake. Just like the pup, the woman might look small and fragile, but she was stronger than she appeared. Her grip would do a lumberjack proud.

"I'm Erin Weber. I own Precious Pets." Brutus started squirming, so Erin put the puppy down. The furball immediately trotted over and tugged on Trent's shoelaces.

"Hey, mutt, cut it out," he said.

"Brutus might not be a pedigree, but he's hardly a mutt," Erin defended. "He's a rescue."

"I didn't mean mutt in a negative way."

"Mutt is a word that has no positive connotations," she countered. "Even though he's from the animal shelter, Brutus has a great deal of dignity." Trent grinned as he watched the pup chew on the shoelaces of his best boots. "Is that a fact? He has dignity?"

Erin frowned. "Of course."

Trent tried to wipe the grin off his face, but the dang thing refused to budge. "I'll keep that in mind."

There was a loud rapping on the front door, then Delia hollered, "Have you arrested her yet?"

Erin frowned. "Who's that?"

"Delia Haverhill. Do you know her?"

"Yes. I met her last weekend. Who does she want you to arrest?"

Brutus had settled down on one of Trent's shoes, apparently to take a nap, so Trent bent down and scooped him up. The dog panted and yipped at him and looked like he might leak from either end, so Trent handed Brutus back to Erin.

"Arrest her, Trent. Do it right now," Delia continued hollering through the door. "How dare she take Pookie!"

Erin was staring at the door to her shop, obviously befuddled. "Um, what does she—"

Trent blew out a sigh. "I'm afraid Delia wants me to arrest you for stealing her Pookie."

ERIN COULDN'T HAVE HEARD THIS MAN CORRECTLY. There was absolutely no way she could have heard him correctly. No one had a reason to want her arrested.

Pushing away her initial panic, she politely asked, "Excuse me? Did you say you're arresting me?"

Trent Barrett smiled, a slow, sexy, lady-killer smile. Erin absolutely refused to react to his smile. Her days of falling for handsome but unreliable men were over. So what if he was tall, with deep-black hair and the most amazing blue eyes? He wasn't her type. Nope. Not at all.

And even if he was her type—which he wasn't—she could hardly be attracted to a man who might arrest her.

"I said Delia wants me to arrest you, but I'm only here to ask a couple of questions," he explained.

The woman outside the front door banged on the glass again. "I'm serious, Trent; I expect results."

Confrontation in any form always made Erin uncomfortable—at least it used to. But since her wedding day fiasco, she'd worked hard at becoming more assertive. These days, she really tried to stand up for herself. She couldn't imagine what she had done to Delia Haverhill that had made her so angry, but Erin wasn't about to be intimidated either by the handsome chief of police or the irate woman outside.

"Look, Chief Barrett—"

"Trent," he said.

Erin shook her head. "No, I'll call you Chief Barrett, if you don't mind."

Once again, he flashed a flirty grin that Erin suspected usually reduced any female within a two-mile radius into a fluttery mass of jelly. Too bad for the chief that she was now flutter-proof. Okay, not one hundred percent flutter-proof but close to it.

"So, Chief Barrett, whatever Delia thinks I've done, I haven't. I have never broken the law."

"I appreciate that, Ms. Weber. Delia is upset about Pookie."

Erin took a deep, calming breath and tried again. "You said that pookie thing before. What in the world is a pookie?"

He chuckled, the sound deep and inviting, but Erin ignored it. Well, tried to, and came pretty darn close.

"Pookie is the name of Delia's plastic rabbit which used to reside in her garden and is now sitting in front of your store. Delia seems to think you had something to do with Pookie's relocation."

"That's the silliest thing I've ever heard. I have no idea what you're talking about. Let me put Brutus in his carrier, then I want to see this Pookie."

Trent nodded. "Seems like the best approach, but I'll warn you, Delia's a trifle hot under the collar. I'm going to head on outside and give her a couple of pointers on police protocol."

Erin had to ask, "Such as?"

"Mostly that she's not allowed to scream and yell while you and I are chatting."

"I don't think you should call interrogating me about a plastic rabbit chatting, Chief."

"I don't think you should call what I'm going to be doing interrogating, Ms. Weber."

Erin didn't want to soften toward Trent Barrett, for a lot of reasons, but she had to admit, he hadn't done anything too terrible. At least not so far.

"I'll put Brutus in his carrier and be outside in a sec," she repeated, not as nervous as she'd been before.

"I'll go talk to Delia."

Although Brutus didn't appreciate being put into his dog carrier, he accepted his fate with as much good grace as a feisty puppy could manage. Then Erin smoothed her green T-shirt that read Precious Pets and her beige slacks.

She took a series of calming breaths following the techniques she'd read about to reduce tension and said the affirmations the book had advised: "You're powerful. You're strong. You're filled with energy."

Then she headed to the front door, her steps decisive, her head held high. She'd just moved to this town and opened her business. Sure, the people of Honey didn't know her. But she wasn't a thief, and Delia Haverhill was about to learn that fact.

Feeling ready, Erin stepped outside and noticed two things—first, that Trent must have had a really intense talking to with Delia, because the older woman had her mouth clamped shut and looked about to explode.

And second, she noticed that Pookie was one sad and sorry-looking plastic bunny rabbit.

Going on the offensive, Erin said to Delia, "I'm so sorry about what happened to you, but I didn't take your rabbit. I have no idea how it came to be in front of my store. But I'm glad you found it and can put it back in your garden."

Delia continued to glare. "If you didn't put it there, who did?"

"Ah, but if I'd stolen it, why would I display it in

front of my store where you'd readily see it? Wouldn't I hide Pookie so I could keep him?"

A tiny fragment of doubt crossed the older woman's face. Erin knew Delia was now a little less sure.

"Delia," Trent said softly. "Remember what we talked about before you say anything."

Delia eventually made a noise that sounded like "hmmrrphfft" but didn't say anything else. Erin frankly couldn't tell if that was a good hmmrrphfft or a bad hmmrrphfft, but at least Delia had stopped demanding that Erin be arrested.

Now Erin turned her attention to Trent, needing his help to solve this mystery. "Honestly, I have no idea how that statue—"

"Pookie," Delia said. "His name is Pookie."

Erin nodded. "Right. Pookie. Well, anyway, I have no idea how Pookie came to be in front of my store."

"You have to know something," Delia said. "Did you see anyone lurking around?"

"Delia," Trent said again, raising one eyebrow and giving the woman a look that Erin could only call marginally polite. "I'm sure if Ms. Weber had seen anyone lurking, she would have called the police whether or not they'd been carrying a pookie."

"Hmmrrphfft," Delia said again.

"You didn't notice Pookie outside when you came to work this morning?" Trent asked.

Erin only wished she had. Although, truthfully, even if she had seen Pookie, she probably wouldn't have called the police to report a plastic bunny. "I didn't see it because I live in the apartment above my shop. I don't come in through the front door. I come down the back stairs."

While Trent wrote a few things in a small notebook, Erin looked at Delia. She felt sorry for the older woman. Delia was obviously very upset. "Delia, I want you to know I would never steal Pookie. I know what it's like to have people take things that belong to you. I can imagine how upset you were when you discovered Pookie missing. He's such an...er...um, attractive rabbit. He must bring you a great deal of joy."

Delia's expression softened, but just a minuscule amount. She still pretty much looked like she wanted Erin beheaded.

"Yes, Pookie is dear to me," Delia said.

Erin reached out and patted the battered plastic animal. "He's sweet. You must have missed him."

Delia held the statue close. "He is sweet, which is why someone stole him."

Erin deliberately ignored the baiting tone in the woman's voice. Instead, she said, "I'm so glad you got him back. When I was in first grade, one of the boys stole my lunch box, which I loved. I was devastated. I ran home and cried and cried."

Delia's expression softened a little more around the edges. "What kind of lunch box was it?"

"Scooby-Doo. And I loved that lunch box. I was so proud of it. I couldn't believe it was gone."

Delia nodded. "Scooby-Doo is a good choice. So, did you get the lunch box back?"

"No. Although I knew who took it, no one would believe me. My parents said I'd probably lost it on the bus and wouldn't buy me another because they felt I'd been careless. My teacher said I'd probably lost it at home somewhere and didn't believe me when I said Billy Porter had stolen it."

"You poor thing," Delia said, patting her on the arm.

"The worst part was that a couple of months later, Billy started coming to school carrying the Scooby-Doo lunch box. I could even see where he'd marked out my name and written his own. I was so upset, but no one would do anything, so I had to ignore it. But it was hard to ignore since Billy liked to tease me by saying 'Don't you wish you had a lunch box as nice as mine?'"

"That rat," Delia huffed. "Someone should have taught that boy a lesson."

Erin looked Delia directly in the eye. "I agree. What Billy did was horrible. That's why I would never, ever take something that didn't belong to me. As you can tell, I still to this day remember the Scooby-Doo lunch box incident."

Delia patted her arm again. "You poor thing."

Trent cleared his throat. "Excuse me. but, Ms. Weber, do you have any idea who might have left Pookie outside your store?"

Delia spun around and glared at him, her hands on her wide hips. "Trent Barrett, have you no manners?"

Both Trent and Erin looked at each other. He seemed as baffled by Delia's comment as she was.

Trent explained. "Delia, I'm trying to find out about Pookie. I thought that was what you wanted me to do."

Delia pointed one finger at him. "You should have sympathized about the lunch box first. Then you can ask about Pookie."

Trent turned to Erin, his deep-blue eyes sparkling

with humor. She could tell he was trying hard not to smile. To his credit, he managed to look sincere when he said, "My deepest apologies," he said. "I'm so sorry to hear about your loss."

"Thank you." Now Erin had to keep from smiling at the mischievous look in Trent's eyes. The man was a flirt, plain and simple. She could tell from the way he was looking at her that he found her attractive.

"Now that I've paid my respects to your lost Scooby-Doo lunch box, do you have any idea how Pookie came to be outside your store?" he asked.

"None at all," she admitted and glanced at Delia. "I really am sorry this happened to you."

Delia patted her arm yet again. "I appreciate your concern. And I realize now that you couldn't possibly have had anything to do with Pookie's disappearance. Not when you've suffered yourself. Trent will have to figure out who really did it."

Erin was relieved the other woman believed her. Not only would she hate to think someone blamed her for a theft, but it wouldn't do Precious Pets any good if everyone started thinking badly of her.

"I'm not done asking questions," Trent said to Delia.

Delia shook her head. "No more questions. She didn't do it. Enough said. Go on back to your office and arrest someone else. I'm going to visit with Erin for a bit." She glanced at the store. "Do you let the local shelters list dogs and cats so they can find forever homes? I didn't pay that much attention when I was here with my grandson last Saturday. You remember Zach, don't you?"

Erin smiled. It would be difficult to forget the eight-year-old. He'd asked a million questions while Delia had visited with the mayor and his wife.

"Yes, I remember Zach. Yes, I help the local animal shelter find homes for the strays. A couple times a month, they bring a few of their pets here to see if my customers are interested in adopting. And then sometimes, I act as a foster home to a kitten or a puppy. Right now, I'm taking care of a puppy named Brutus. He's a sweetie and needs a good home."

"Let me take a look at him. Also, do you sell birdseed? I have a new bird feeder that looks like the Tower of Pisa. I need to stock it."

Erin smiled, relaxing for the first time since this whole mess had started. Even though she knew all along that she hadn't done a thing wrong, just the threat of being arrested made her jittery and jumpy. She was used to always being the good girl. The good daughter. The good student. The good fiancée.

She wouldn't know how to be bad if someone gave her lessons.

"I have several types of birdseed," Erin told Delia, thrilled the woman was now being friendly. "I'm certain I have something that will work for you."

She turned to look at the handsome chief of police. Her pulse rate picked up, but she ignored it. Even Pookie, the plastic bunny rabbit statue, was smart enough to know a man like Trent Barrett was trouble.

"Are we done?" she asked him.

He grinned, his look downright flirtatious. His blue eyes sparkled once again with mischief, and Erin's first instinct was to smile back at him. Thankfully, her common sense kicked in, and she stopped herself.

Smiling at Trent struck her as an activity only a tiny bit less dangerous than carrying around a lit stick of dynamite. The man was a handsome devil all right.

When she didn't return his smile, he only grinned bigger. She could tell he found her amusing, but she didn't care. She wasn't going to flirt with this man no matter how tempting it might be.

"You're no longer a suspect in Pookie's kidnapping," Trent finally said. "But I'd say we're far from done."

With that and a goodbye to Delia, he walked away. Erin frowned. What did he mean by that crack that they were far from done?

"Woo-wee, that boy is a charmer. All of those Barrett boys are," Delia said as they watched Trent Barrett leave. "But that one, he's a flirt through and through. A mighty fine-looking man, but a flirt, that's for sure."

"Mmm." Erin didn't want to discuss Trent Barrett. The man made her...pensive. And pensive could be bad for her emotional health.

Delia yanked open the door to the shop and headed straight for the birdseed. "You have a wonderful selection."

"Thanks." Erin helped her pick just the right type for the birds she wanted to attract. Then after introducing Delia to Brutus, she rang up the older woman's order.

"Sure you don't want to adopt this puppy? He's a great little fellow," Erin tried, even though Delia had already made it clear she thought Brutus was way too active.

"Brutus isn't right for me. Does he have any sisters?"

Erin hid her disappointment. Delia wasn't the first person to ask that. So far, Erin had sent three people to the county animal shelter to see Brutus' sisters.

Well, an adopted animal was one more with a home, so Erin told Delia, "Yes. The shelter has several females left from the litter."

Delia eyed Brutus, who was now gnawing on Erin's sneaker. "Yes, I think one of the girls might suit me better. I'll go over there this afternoon."

Erin reached down and detached Brutus from her shoe, telling him firmly, "No, Brutus." Then she said to Delia, "I'm sure you'll find a wonderful dog to love."

"I'm sure I will, too." Just as the older woman was about to leave, she said, "Hon, before I go, I wanted to say I'm so sorry about the mix-up this morning. I only hope Trent finds the people who stole Pookie. They deserve to be in jail."

"I'm sure the chief will do a thorough investigation," Erin assured her.

"You're probably right. Even though he's something of a rogue, Trent's good at his job. He keeps this town running smoothly." She leaned forward a little and added, "But just so you know, be very careful if you decide to go out with him. That man breaks hearts as easily as I crack eggs."

Erin handed Delia the bag with the birdseed and said as much to herself as to the other woman, "I'm not worried. My heart is unbreakable."

"Dang it, Leigh, stop yanking on my arm. I told you, I already met Erin Weber. Last week."

Trent's sister made a snorting noise and kept tugging. "You tried to arrest her. That doesn't count. Now come on and meet her the right way, without the threat of imprisonment hanging over her head. You'll love Erin. She's in my pottery class."

Trent stopped and refused to let his sister tow him any farther. "You're in a pottery class?"

Leigh rolled her eyes. "Jeez, you're easily distracted. Okay, yes, I'm taking a pottery class."

Trent shuddered. "Just the thought of you around all that fragile stuff makes me cringe."

"Very funny, bozo. Now come on. I want you to meet Erin the right way."

Trent groaned. He and his brothers had developed almost a sixth sense over the years when it came to Leigh and her evil plans. This little visit to meet Erin

Weber had "Leigh plot" written all over it. She was up to something as sure as snakes liked to slither.

"Don't even think about it," he told her.

"Don't even think about what?"

"Whatever scheme you've got cooking in your devious mind. I'm not falling for it."

"I have no idea what you're talking about. I'm not up to anything. I just want you to meet a friend of mine." Leigh tried to look innocent, but he didn't buy it for a second.

"You're guilty all right."

Leigh put her hands on her hips. "I am not guilty. Besides, you can't prove a thing."

"Now there's a comment seldom made by an innocent person."

Leigh snorted again and started walking toward the pet shop. "You know, Chase and Nathan aren't nearly as suspicious as you are. They believe me when I tell them things."

"Well, that's only because they're not paying attention these days." Boy, that was the understatement of the year. Chase had recently married the town's librarian, and he and Megan were blissful honeymooners. And Nathan was engaged to Emma, a woman Leigh knew from college.

Suddenly, like a whack to the head, Trent understood Leigh's plan.

"You're trying to fix me up," he accused.

Leigh laughed. "As if. I like Erin. Why would I want to ruin her life by getting her mixed up with you?"

Even though he didn't care for her tone, his sister had a point. Not about the ruining-this-woman's-life stuff, but the thought behind it. Leigh, like everyone else in town, knew he wasn't the type to settle down. He liked to enjoy life, and as far as he was concerned, love was for saps.

If Erin really was a friend of Leigh's, she wouldn't try to fix them up. Leigh had never tried to fix any of her friends up with him.

Even Leigh wasn't that evil.

They'd reached Precious Pets, so Trent held the door for his sister. She rewarded him by leaning up and giving him a quick kiss on the cheek.

"You're my favorite brother," she said. "Now be nice, or I'll kick your butt."

He made the snorting noise Leigh was so fond of and said her favorite phrase, "As if."

"It's true."

"Oops, watch out for Brutus," Erin called from inside.

Trent looked down just in time to see the furball making a break. He scooped up the dog seconds before the rascal made it out the open door. Giving the pup his most serious look, he said, "Hold it, mister. You're under arrest."

"Better Brutus than me," said Erin, coming over to take the puppy from Trent. As he handed over Brutus, their hands brushed. He couldn't resist prolonging the contact a little longer than necessary. She gave him a startled look, then took the puppy and stepped back. He smiled. Dang. The woman might not like him, but she sure wasn't immune to him.

"Trent's here to tell you how sorry he is for trying to arrest you," Leigh said.

Trent frowned at his sister. "No, I'm not. I'm here because you dragged me here." He glanced at Erin. "Not that it isn't a pleasure to see you again, Ms. Weber."

"You can call me Erin now that you're no longer threatening to arrest me."

"Erin. And for the record, I didn't threaten to arrest you. I said Delia wanted me to arrest you. I only intended on asking you a few questions."

"Have you found out who stole Pookie yet?" she asked.

Leigh hooted a laugh. "Pookie. I still can't get over that Delia names those plastic statues in her yard. What does she call the armadillo she's got out by the tree?"

"His name is Stanley. And the turtle statue she's got in her flowerbed is Dazzle," Erin said.

"You and Delia seem to have hit it off despite her wanting me to arrest you," Trent pointed out.

"Delia has stopped by a couple times in the last week. We've had a chance to talk. She's very nice. She adopted one of Brutus' sisters and has been coming in for supplies," Erin said, heading toward a crate with Brutus.

"Leave him out," Leigh said. "Let him visit with us."

Erin set the dog down. "Okay, but we need to watch him. He's a sneaky guy."

Trent raised an eyebrow when Brutus came over and started chewing on the side of his shoe. "Hey, cut that out."

When the dog didn't stop, Trent looked at Erin. "What's with the furball and shoes?"

Erin sighed. "His chewing fascination isn't limited to shoes. He'll pretty much chomp on anything that slows down. I'm working on breaking his bad habits, but he's a scallywag and isn't coming around easily."

"Sounds like a male I'd be related to." Leigh reached down and scratched Brutus. "What this guy needs is a home with someone who's as much a rascal as he is, don't you, fella?"

Brutus yapped, almost as if he were agreeing with Leigh. His sister laughed. "See, he thinks I'm right."

"Unfortunately, I haven't had any luck finding him a home. The people at the shelter suggested I bring Brutus back and see if I can place a different animal, but I can't give up on Brutus. Not yet."

As soon as Leigh stopped scratching Brutus, he returned to chewing on one of Trent's shoes.

"Dang it, dog," Trent said. "I mean it. Cut it out."

Brutus yapped again and resumed chewing.

"He obviously thinks your shoe is a bark-o-lounger," Leigh teased.

Trent groaned. "Bad joke."

"Brutus liked it, didn't you, sweetie?" Leigh leaned over and picked up the puppy. "You need a wonderful home with someone who understands the male mind. Someone who's had a lot of experience with wild impulses." She grinned at Trent over the top of the puppy's head. "Someone like my brother."

Erin hadn't realized Leigh's brother liked dogs. In fact, looking at the frown on his face at this very moment, she still wasn't sure he liked dogs. He was staring at his sister like she'd just announced he should adopt a rattlesnake.

But before he could protest, Erin gave him her best smile and pushed her advantage. "Would you really consider adopting Brutus? That would be wonderful. I don't want to take him back to the shelter, and I live in the small apartment over the store, so I can't adopt him."

Trent sighed and shook his head. "Leigh was joking. I can't adopt him."

Disappointment flooded through Erin. Something awful could happen to Brutus if he didn't find a home. "Are you sure? He's actually a sweet little guy."

At that moment, Brutus started gnawing on the collar of Leigh's blouse.

"Seems to me he's more like a one-man demolition team," Trent said dryly.

"Oh, come on, Trent," Leigh said. "He's no worse than you were when you were young. And look how you've settled down." She totally undermined her statement by laughing when she finished. "Well, sort of settled down. At least now you're less likely to be caught."

Normally, Erin wouldn't press someone on a decision like this, but despite his teasing of Brutus, Trent had been kind to the puppy, and she was frantic. The animal shelter might put Brutus to sleep.

She scanned her mind for some way to convince Trent to take the puppy. The best she could come up with was, "He's young, yet. He'll calm down with age."

Trent was frowning. Frowning a lot. "I'm not the sort for a puppy. I'm not home much."

"I'll help you take care of him," Leigh offered. "I can stop by while you're at work and play with him and walk him."

Rather than looking pleased by his sister's offer,

Trent continued frowning. "I'm not interested in adopting a puppy. Thanks for asking, Leigh."

"I'll buy the food," Leigh said, upping her offer.

"No," Trent said.

"I'll pay for all the shots."

"No."

Since Leigh was striking out, Erin made the only other offer that came to mind.

"I'll help you train him," she said. "I'll throw in free puppy-training lessons. A class starts in a few days, and there's room for you to join."

Leigh tapped him on the arm. "Now how can you pass up free puppy-training lessons given by Erin? By the time she's done, Brutus will be better behaved than a choirboy. And who knows? Maybe you'll learn a thing or two about behaving."

Trent continued frowning at his sister.

Erin quickly pressed on. "Yes, Brutus will learn how to behave. And after you have him neutered, he'll—"

"Whoa, whoa. Hold it right there," Trent said. "Neutered?"

Erin mentally crossed her fingers, hoping Trent wasn't going to be difficult about this. She gave him a reassuring smile, but he looked positively horrified.

"The shelter won't let you adopt Brutus unless you agree to have him neutered," Erin explained. "They'll do the operation there at a discount, or you can take him to your own vet and have it done."

As she watched, Trent seemed to pale beneath his tan. "Neutered?" he repeated.

Leigh snorted and cuddled Brutus. "Stop acting like someone is trying to do it to you. Of course, the puppy has to be neutered. You can't contribute to animal over-population. But look at it this way, Brutus is going to live a long and happy life in the comfort of your home. Isn't that a fair trade-off?"

Erin thought so, too, but Trent turned his head and glared at his sister. "Not in my book, it isn't," he said. When Leigh snorted again, he added defensively, "It's a male thing. You wouldn't understand."

"Oh, let it go," Leigh said. "We're talking about the dog, not you. And you have to save this poor dog's life. If he goes back to the shelter, he may be put to sleep."

Erin took a step closer to Trent. He turned and looked at her. Wow. His eyes were so incredibly blue. Amazingly blue.

For a second, she just stood there looking at Trent. Then Leigh nudged her. Hard.

"Isn't that true, Erin? Couldn't poor, unfortunate Brutus end up being put to sleep if no brave person steps forward and adopts him?"

Erin nodded. "Yes. But Trent, if you really don't want to adopt Brutus, then you shouldn't. You should adopt a pet because you want to love them, not because you're forced into it."

Leigh dismissed her comment with the wave of one hand. "Trent, don't listen to Erin. She's trying to be nice. But I'm telling you right now, it's your moral duty to adopt this puppy."

Trent raised one eyebrow. "My moral duty? I don't think so."

"Sure it is. If you don't save him from the puppy gallows, how will you sleep?"

Now that was laying it on a bit thick. Erin figured

Leigh had pushed her brother about as far as a person could be pushed. She wasn't surprised when Trent made a sound that was almost a growl. "Stop talking, Leigh."

Leigh held Brutus out in front of Trent. "Look at his face. Look at his sweet puppy eyes. Can't you see he's begging you to adopt him?" When Trent continued to frown at her, Leigh said in a high, squeaky voice, "Please, Mr. Trent, please adopt me and give me a home. I'll be a good puppy. Every morning, I'll fetch your paper—"

"I don't subscribe to the paper," Trent said flatly.

"Then I'll bring you your slippers—"

"I don't wear slippers."

Now Leigh was frowning right back at Trent. "Fine. Then I'll answer your phone."

Trent sighed.

"Leigh, if he doesn't want to—" Erin said at the same time that Trent said, "Okay."

Erin froze and looked at him. "What did you say?"

Trent reached out and patted Brutus. "I said okay. I've been convinced. I'll adopt the furball."

With a loud, "Wahoo," Leigh danced around with Brutus, singing him an off-tune song and making up words to rhyme with his name. "Brutus is the Cutest" was okay. "Brutus is the Rootest" didn't make much sense. And "Brutus is the Dooest" sounded totally bizarre.

Trent looked at Leigh, then glanced at Erin. "You don't by any chance know someone who wants to adopt a sister, do you? She's almost housebroken."

With another snort, Leigh leaned over and gave

Trent a loud, smacking kiss on the cheek. "Har-de-har-har. You're so funny. I can't stop laughing."

"I'm serious," he told her, but even Erin didn't believe him for one second. For starters, he was smiling at his sister. And then there was the fact that he took Brutus from Leigh and carefully cradled the dog as he walked over to the pet food section of the store.

"What does the furball eat?"

Erin studied the man before her. Trent Barrett might be a world-class flirt, but he was also one heck of a nice guy. The flirt part was easy to resist. The nice guy part made her nervous. Very, very nervous. A nice guy who loved his sister and was sweet enough to adopt an admittedly rowdy puppy could prove tempting, especially to a woman who'd been on her own for a very long time.

"So what does he eat?" Trent repeated, turning to look at Erin.

She cleared her suddenly tight throat, and a slow, lazy grin crossed Trent's face. He knew she'd been thinking nice things about him. She frowned, and he laughed.

"Come on over here, Erin. I won't bite," he said in a deep, beguiling voice.

"Don't count on it." Leigh walked over and rapped her brother on the arm. "I wouldn't put much past this yahoo."

Rather than appearing offended, Trent continued to grin at Erin. "Maybe the lady would like to find out for herself what I'm capable of doing."

Oh, no. No, no, no. The lady was most definitely not interested in anything this handsome devil had in mind. Erin mentally erased every single nice thing she'd thought about Trent. He wasn't a sweet guy. He was a flirt.

"Thanks, but no thanks," she said coolly.

A nice guy might have tempted her, but a flirt she could resist.

TRENT EYED HIS NEW PUPPY, WHO WAS HAPPILY chasing his own tail on the floor of the family room. He'd brought the dog home yesterday, and he still couldn't get Brutus to do a single thing he told him to do.

"That's one dumb dog," Trent said. "What does he think is going to happen when he catches his tail?"

"He's not dumb," Leigh maintained, nudging the pup so he'd leave his tail alone. "First off, he's only a puppy. Second off, he's your puppy, so a little pity wouldn't be out of place."

"Real cute," Trent said, settling back in his chair. "It's your fault he's my puppy."

"You always said you wanted a dog." Leigh patted Brutus.

"A dog, Leigh. I wanted a dog. Not something that looks like it should be vacuumed up."

Leigh laughed and looked at Brutus. "Mean old Trent. He's saying bad things about you. But you ignore him. He's just grumpy because Erin didn't like it when he flirted with her."

Trent groaned. "I didn't flirt with her. I was only being nice."

"Ha! No, you weren't. You flirted with her, and she didn't melt like butter on a hot sidewalk, and you're not used to that, so now you're in a bad mood. I took Intro to Psychology. I know how people work."

Trent would give anything to tell Leigh she was wrong, but dang it, she was right. At least sort of right. He was annoyed that Erin had blown him off. And the lady had. Big time. After his remark about not biting, she'd treated him like he had some highly contagious disease.

Not that he was vain, but ladies usually liked him. A lot. But even though he could tell Erin was attracted to him, he could also tell she didn't like him. And that bothered the hell out of him.

"Knock, knock," called a feminine voice from the front hall. Trent groaned. Great. Now his brother Chase and his new wife, Megan, were here. He could just imagine what Leigh was going to tell them.

"You won't guess what's been happening," Leigh said the second Megan and Chase entered the family room.

Chase grinned. "I'll take a shot in the dark. One of you got a dog."

"How did you ever guess?" Trent asked dryly.

"I'm psychic about some things," Chase said. When Brutus scurried over and flopped on one of his boots, he leaned down and scratched the puppy behind the ears. "This sure is a bitty thing." He tipped his head and looked at Trent. "Can't be your dog because it's way too delicate."

"Hey." Leigh came over and picked Brutus up. "Brutus is not a delicate dog. He weighs almost five pounds. He'll be over ten when he's fully grown."

Chase leaned down and eyed the dog cuddled in his sister's arms. "Oh, yeah? Then I take back what I said. He's a terrifying monster."

Megan moved over and patted Brutus. "I think he's adorable. Is he yours, Leigh?"

"Nope. Trent adopted him."

"Had he seen the dog before he adopted it?" Chase asked.

When Leigh bobbed her head, he laughed. "Now why do I get the feeling an attractive lady appears somewhere in this story."

"Stop teasing poor Trent," Megan said kindly. Trent knew he liked his brother's wife. She was nothing like the members of his family.

Chase kissed his wife and told her, "Not possible, sweetheart. Teasing him is my job as his big brother."

Trent decided he'd had enough. He walked over to Leigh, taking Brutus out of her arms. "I think I'll let the furball run in the backyard."

"Make sure the Wharton's cat isn't out. Fluffy could make a meal out of Brutus," Chase said with a chuckle.

"Funny. You and Leigh are such comedians." Trent opened the back door and let Brutus scamper out. Then he followed him. He might as well go play with the furball since his family was more aggravating than a rash. They weren't going to stop teasing until they left to go home. "For your information, I adopted Brutus because I like him."

Chase and Megan followed him outside. Chase dropped his arm around Trent's shoulders. "I've been to the pet shop. I've met Erin Weber. She's very nice and very pretty. And you, well, you are you."

Trent shoved away from his brother, not wanting to talk about this. "I adopted Brutus because I like him," he repeated.

Megan walked over to stand next to him. "Of course, you do. Brutus is a very..." Her voice drifted off, and Trent followed the direction of her gaze. As he watched, Brutus attacked a blade of grass. The annoying part was that in this battle of brains and brawn, the grass seemed to be winning.

After a couple of seconds watching the dog and the grass, Megan said, "Brutus is a very interesting puppy. I can see why you adopted him."

"It had nothing to do with Erin," Trent maintained, wishing there were even a sliver of truth in that statement.

"Of course, it didn't," Megan said sweetly, but Trent was fairly sure even she didn't believe him. "I think it was a wonderful thing you did. Especially since you threatened to arrest the poor woman."

"What?" How in the world did the truth get so twisted? "I didn't threaten to arrest her. I went to her store to ask her some questions."

Chase hooted a laugh. "I can imagine what sort of questions."

"Don't be ridiculous," Trent said. "Erin's a nice woman, but she's not my type."

"I thought your type was breathing," Chase said.

Trent sighed. His family was wrong. Dead wrong. He hadn't adopted Brutus because he found Erin attractive. She had nothing to do with this decision. He'd adopted Brutus because he liked dogs. Dogs offered you companionship. Dogs offered you affection. Dogs offered you protection.

A loud commotion by the fence drew his attention.

"Dang it, Fluffy. Put Brutus down."

Jeez, what kind of dog couldn't hold his own against a skinny, eighteen-year-old cat?

TRENT LOOKED AT THE WOODEN BIRDHOUSE SITTING next to the back door of Precious Pets.

"It looks like the Leaning Tower of Pisa," he said.

"When I saw it, I couldn't believe someone would leave it out in plain sight," said Joe Rafton, one of his newer officers. "You'd think the thief would have more sense. When Delia reported it stolen, I figured we'd never find it. But there it is. Big as life."

Trent nodded. Yeah, he'd figured they'd never find the birdhouse. But here it was. Outside Erin's shop. Just like Pookie had been. Only this time, the stolen article was outside the back door rather than the front. Still, it was in plain sight for anyone to see.

Of course, he didn't for a second believe that Erin was responsible for this. He couldn't say why, but he trusted her. Not to mention, a person would have to be phenomenally stupid to leave a purloined article sitting outside in plain view.

No, someone was up to something.

"You want me to question the owner of the pet shop?" Joe asked.

Trent should. He definitely should let Joe talk to Erin. But Joe's wife was going to deliver their first child any day now, and his shift was almost over.

"I'll talk to her," Trent said.

Joe didn't even try to cover his surprise. "Gee, Chief, isn't this kind of below you?"

"Course not. Besides, Delia Haverhill got me started on this case when she insisted I arres—question Erin when the first stolen item appeared outside the pet store."

Joe scratched his jaw, obviously hiding a smile. "Do you think Erin knows who is doing this?"

Trent ignored the bait. "No. She'd tell me if she did." He was positive about that.

"What I can't figure out is, who in Honey would do such a thing? We've never had this kind of trouble before."

Joe was right. Something this strange had never happened in Honey. But it sure was happening now, and Trent needed to let Erin know what was going on.

He knocked loudly on the back door of the shop and waited for her to answer. As soon as she opened the door, she frowned.

"You have that chief-of-police look on your face. Are you here to arrest me again?"

Boy, that really fried his bacon. What had he ever done to this woman that would make her think so badly of him? After all, he hadn't actually arrested her. Didn't that count for something?

He took a great deal of pleasure in explaining, "Of course I'm not here to arrest you."

Her expression brightened. "Good. So why are you here? Is it about Brutus?"

"No. I need to ask you a couple of questions about

this birdhouse." He nodded to the lopsided structure next to the door.

Erin came outside and looked at the birdhouse. "I don't believe it. That birdhouse belongs to Delia."

He hadn't been expecting her to know who the owner was. "How do you know that?"

She maintained eye contact as she said, "Delia told us about it the last time you were here in an official capacity. She said it looks like the Leaning Tower of Pisa, so that has to be hers. How many people in town have one shaped like that?"

Hopefully only one. "I haven't spoken to Delia yet, so I don't know for a fact that it's hers," he said. "But it sounds like the item she reported stolen this morning. Let me get her over here to take a look at it."

Erin sighed loudly. "Fine. But I'm sure it's hers. What I can't figure out is why someone is doing this."

"The things people do often don't make sense," Joe tossed out. "Look at Pet Rocks. No one ever understood them."

Trent let Joe's example slide. "Don't worry about it, Erin. We'll figure out who's doing this and why."

"This really bothers me," she said. "Everyone in town is going to hate me."

"Naw," said Joe. "Honey is a nice town. We rarely hate anyone. We sometimes dislike a few. Like if they consistently litter. Or maybe don't mow their lawn very often. Or take up too many parking spaces at the grocery store. But other than things like that, we're nice to everyone."

Erin didn't seem a bit comforted by Joe's assurance.

She looked at Trent. "Will you figure it out before an angry mob shows up on my doorstep?"

"We don't have a lot of torch-bearing villagers around here," Trent told her.

Joe rocked back and forth on the balls of his feet. "Too bad we can't get a mob together. They could watch your store and find out who's responsible."

In his own way, Joe was onto something. Maybe they could set up a video camera. In the meantime, Trent planned on keeping a close watch on Erin's store. Sooner or later, he'd catch the culprit.

"I only hope Delia doesn't go back to wanting me arrested," Erin said, her tone and posture dejected.

"She won't," Trent assured her. "You're still getting a lot of mileage out of the lunch box story. There's nothing like a good Scooby-Doo story to get a town into your cheering section. So don't worry about it. I'll take care of you."

Erin fixed him with an unwavering gaze. "No. You take care of whoever is stealing these things. I'll take care of myself."

3

"I want to thank everyone for coming to tonight's Dog Behavior Class. I hope you're enjoying your new family members," Erin said.

Trent glanced down at Brutus. Mostly he'd been cleaning up after the furball. Brutus might be tiny, but he had the disposition of a tornado. He'd gnawed on every shoe he'd managed to find, done a terrific job taking bites out of the living room drapes, and chewed the end of the leather sofa until it was mush. Trent had bought him an impressive assortment of chew toys, but the boy ignored them.

All in all, Brutus had made himself a little too much at home.

Glancing at the other members of the class, though, Trent hoped his pet wouldn't be the worst one there. Delia had come to the class, bringing along a sister of Brutus' that seemed pretty calm and respectful. Trent was glad the older woman had come. Her presence proved to everyone in town that she didn't believe Erin had stolen her birdhouse. She, like Trent and his officers, had no idea what was going on. But Delia firmly maintained Erin wasn't at fault. And now that Trent had set up video cameras outside the store, it probably wouldn't be long before they caught the thief.

Besides Delia, there were three more people in the class. The other two women both had puppies that looked like they might be frisky. Karla Ashmore had a spaniel that seemed full of spunk, and Lynn Claude had a boxer who seemed pretty spry as well. No way would Brutus be the worst dog there.

Best of all, the other guy in the class had a German shepherd puppy—a male German shepherd puppy. Trent was positive that bad boy had more than a few behavior problems to iron out. He kept giving the other dogs a nasty look that Brutus apparently took to mean he was about to become an appetizer. One look from the German shepherd, and Brutus hid behind Trent's legs.

"Calm down, furball," Trent said as Brutus continued to hide. Not that he could really blame the puppy. The German shepherd was a big dog. A tough dog.

Trent looked at Brutus, who yipped and sounded like a perfect little princess. Great. Now the mutt even sounded like a delicate princess dog.

"How is everyone doing with housebreaking? Any problems?" Erin smiled at Delia. "Is Muffin getting the hang of it?"

Delia patted her puppy. "Oh, yes. She caught on right away. I followed the instructions in that brochure you gave me, and I didn't have a single problem."

Little Muffin must have known she was being praised, because she practically pranced in place. Trent rolled his eyes. He'd believe Muffin was completely housebroken the day he believed Santa Claus had a cholesterol level under 200.

Trent squatted and gave Brutus a pat. "Like I believe that," he said softly.

Brutus made a doggy snorting noise that Trent took as agreement.

Erin looked at them. "How is Brutus doing with his training?"

In a word? Failing.

But both for his own pride and for Brutus', Trent said, "Good. He's doing a great job."

Doubt crossed Erin's face. "You're sure? Because Brutus might take a little longer to catch on."

Hey, what did she mean by that crack? Brutus might not be as prissy as Muffin, but he wasn't the dumbest dog at the pound. Sure, he was having more accidents than successes, but there was no way Trent was going to admit that to this group. A man had to have some loyalty to his dog, even if it was a furball.

"Brutus is doing just fine," Trent assured her.

Erin smiled. "Good. I'm glad to hear he's doing well. I knew you two would hit it off."

Yeah, like either one of them had had a choice in the matter. Trent looked at the German shepherd again, then at the dog's owner. The man had moved to town a couple of months ago to work at Nathan's company. What was his name? Sam? Stan? Something that started with an *S*.

Erin looked at the man. "So, Sean—"

"Sean. That's it."

Both Sean and Erin looked at him. Trent grinned. "Sorry. Go on."

For several seconds, Erin continued to look at Trent. Obviously, his behavior had her puzzled. He grinned and winked at her, which made her frown and look away.

"So, Sean, how are things going?" Erin asked the other man, but Trent didn't miss the slightly breathless hitch to her voice. Now that was interesting.

"Good," Sean said.

"No problems with Scamp?"

"Scamp?" Trent chuckled, looking at the German shepherd. "Jeez, who names these dogs? Mine should be named Scamp, and the shepherd should be Brutus."

Sean frowned at him. "I picked the name Scamp. I think it suits him."

The German shepherd sat perfectly still next to his owner. There wasn't anything remotely scamp-like about the puppy. Brutus, however, had latched on to the hem of Trent's pants and was playing tug-of-war.

"Cut it out, furball," Trent said absently.

Brutus wagged his tail and continued chewing.

Erin walked over to look at Brutus. "The secret to training your puppy is to be firm and consistent."

Hey, he might not be the best pet parent, but he knew how to follow directions. He was following every blasted rule in that booklet Erin had given him.

"Excuse me, Erin, but I'm consistently firm," Trent said.

The second the words left his mouth, he realized

what he'd said. Dang it. As he expected, Karla laughed, as did Lynn. Karla even winked at him.

Erin neither laughed nor winked at him. She blushed. Bright red. Really bright red. Her reaction made the other ladies laugh even more.

Erin cleared her throat. Then she cleared it again. She briefly glanced at Trent, then quickly looked away. See, that was doubly interesting. For a lady who seemed to have no interest in him, she sure was acting suspicious.

"Let's get started with the lessons," Erin finally said, but her voice was almost as squeaky as Brutus' yip.

Trent would give her credit, though. Over the next hour, she tried to be professional. She did a good job, too, at least when she was talking to the other members of the class. But every single time she came to help him with Brutus, Erin became noticeably flustered. She always kept her gaze focused completely on Brutus. Not once did she make eye contact with him.

He took that as a really encouraging sign. Sean didn't fluster Erin, but he sure did. Good. He wanted to fluster Erin. He liked her. He liked the way her eyes sparkled when she patted Brutus, the way she laughed when the puppy rolled over for her to rub his belly, the way she tried to be so stern when she told him not to lick her face.

"Trent, please tell Brutus to leave Muffin alone," Erin said, interrupting his thoughts.

Trent looked at Brutus, who was chewing on Muffin's collar. He sighed and pulled the dog away from his sister.

"Cut it out, Brutus," Trent said.

Erin shook her head. "You need to tell him no."

"I did tell him no."

Again, she shook her head. "You said cut it out. Brutus needs one word to associate with negative actions."

Trent shrugged. "Fine. No."

Erin finally looked him directly in the face. "Say 'No, Brutus' when you want to correct him."

Trent started to follow her directions, but Erin placed a hand on his arm. "Not now. You only say that when he's doing something you want him to stop."

"That's pretty much all the time," Trent admitted. He looked at her hand on his arm, then glanced back at her face. She pulled her hand back so fast she almost lost her balance.

Trent smiled. He liked the way things were going tonight. He liked it very much. And he especially liked it when after class was over, Erin requested he stay.

Oh, yeah. He liked this a lot.

❧

WHILE SHE SAW THE OTHER STUDENTS OUT, ERIN tried to formulate what she was going to say to Trent. He and Brutus had done badly tonight. Very badly. Horribly, in fact. At this rate, poor Brutus would never develop even the most basic behavior skills. The puppy simply didn't listen to Trent.

And for his part, Trent wasn't learning a heck of a lot either. These two males needed a good talking-to, and she was just the lady to do it.

"Brutus and I are being kept after school, huh?"

Trent teased when Erin returned after seeing the others out.

"Trent, do you think Brutus did well tonight?"

Trent chuckled and pointed at the dog. Brutus was happily chewing on Trent's right shoe. "The whole concept of good behavior seems lost on this fellow."

"I refuse to believe that. Brutus can be trained to behave, just like any animal can be trained."

Trent slowly shook his head. "I'm not sure I agree with you, Erin. Not all animals take to training. Some like staying wild and free. I think Brutus may be a fellow who refuses to settle down."

Erin studied Trent. From what Delia and the other ladies in town had told her, Trent also was one of those animals who refused to settle down. He probably wasn't the best person to train Brutus. Trent had a life's-short-have-fun attitude. For all she knew, he wasn't doing much to try to train Brutus. Heck, maybe he didn't even want to train the puppy.

"Brutus could be a very nice dog if you train him," she said, wanting Trent and the puppy to be happy together. To prove her point, she looked at Brutus. "No, Brutus."

Brutus stopped chewing on Trent's shoe, and Erin smiled. "See? Just a little training is all he needs."

Before she could truly savor the thrill of victory, Brutus trotted over and started chewing on her right shoe instead. Trent laughed loudly.

"Oh, yeah, I can see how trainable he is. You have the boy firmly under control."

Erin reached down and extricated the dog from her

shoe. Or rather her shoe from the dog. Then she placed Brutus on the floor and sat next to him.

"Brutus," she said, wanting the puppy to focus on her.

The dog wagged his tail. That was a good sign. He definitely knew his name. When he looked at her, she said firmly, "Sit, Brutus."

Brutus wagged his tail some more.

Erin sighed. This wasn't going to be easy. Some dogs took to training readily. Others needed a little extra help.

And in Brutus' case, he might need a lot of extra help.

"Brutus kinda barks to a different drummer," Trent said, sitting next to Erin. Brutus immediately scurried over and flopped on Trent's lap. When the dog rolled over on his back, Trent good-naturedly scratched his stomach.

"Any ideas what I might try with the furball here?" Trent asked, smiling at Erin. "Believe it or not, I do want the boy to have at least a few manners. How's he going to impress the ladies if he's uncouth?"

Wow. This close up, she could see how amazingly blue Trent's eyes were. He certainly was one gorgeous man. Good thing she was immune to gorgeous, flirtatious men because she'd probably be falling under his spell right now if she wasn't.

Of course, her heart was racing, but that had nothing to do with Trent being so close. Sure, her breathing was on the rapid side, but that also had nothing to do with Trent. Not a single thing.

"Hello? Erin? You still with me?" Trent teased.

Erin mentally shook herself and said, "Of course. I was thinking about your question. I'm trying to decide what's the best way to train Brutus."

Trent's expression made it clear he didn't believe a word she was saying. But at least he had the decency not to comment.

"Oh, and remember, Brutus won't need to impress the ladies. You promised to have him fixed."

Trent winced but didn't disagree. Instead, he said, "I have an idea. Why don't I pay you to give Brutus a little extra training? He may do better one-on-one."

Erin had to admit that Trent might be right. Brutus might respond better if he had her complete attention. "Perhaps I can work with him a couple of extra days this week."

Trent was still scratching the dog's belly. "Thanks, because I don't know what I'm doing wrong. I mean, I'm used to training people. Heck, growing up on a ranch, I'm used to training horses, too. But this dog has me baffled."

Erin found Trent's admission endearing. He really was trying to help the puppy.

"Some puppies take a little longer," Erin said. Then because of Trent's admission, she had to make one of her own. "Plus, it's not like I had much luck with Brutus before you adopted him. I hadn't gotten very far with his training."

"Unless you were teaching him to chew on shoes. He's really good at that."

Erin laughed. "Um, no, that wasn't something I taught him. I'm pretty sure Brutus is what you'd call a natural-born chewer."

"I think you're right," Trent said dryly as he removed the cuff of his shirt from Brutus' mouth. "The furball definitely likes to chew."

"I'm sure we can break him of his bad habits," Erin assured Trent, wanting to make certain he didn't become discouraged by Brutus' lack of progress.

"I'll have to take your word on that one."

"Brutus is a smart dog. He'll learn."

"Oh, I'm not denying he's smart," Trent said, moving Brutus when the puppy tried to chew on the pocket of his shirt. "I think he's downright ornery. In my experience, it takes a lot of incentive to get the ornery out of any creature."

"Did it take a lot of incentive for you?" Erin found herself asking without really meaning to do so. But now that she'd asked the question, she discovered she really wanted to know the answer.

Trent's smile turned into a full-fledged lady-killer grin. "Some folks say I still have ornery left in me, but I deny it. I'm about as good as a man can get these days." He patted Brutus' head. "Dang, I even have a furball for a dog. A man can't have much ornery left in him if he lets himself be talked into adopting a puppy like Brutus."

"Maybe not ornery," she conceded, "but I think you definitely have a lot of..."

When she didn't immediately go on, Trent chuckled. "Yes? I have a lot of what?"

"Flirt," she finally said. "You have a lot of flirt in you."

Trent tried to look offended, but Erin ended up laughing at his goofy expression.

"Come on, admit it, you're a flirt. You were flirting with Karla tonight."

"I was not."

"Sure you were."

Trent shook his head. "Nope. Not true. She was flirting with me, but I didn't flirt back. The lady recently left her husband. Personally, I'm hoping they work out their problems and stay together. I would never flirt with a woman who was married, even if she's separated."

Erin could hear sincerity in his voice, see it in his expression. She'd never admit it, but she was glad to hear Trent had rules about these sorts of things. The more time she spent with him, the more she liked Trent. She'd hate to think he'd run around with any woman, regardless of her marital status. "A rogue with a heart," she murmured.

"Naw. I just figure no one has the right to meddle with a married couple. They have to work through any problems on their own. I'm not about to hop into a snake pit like that."

"You consider marriage a snake pit?"

Trent shrugged. "More or less. Some of them I've seen make a snake pit look good."

"You can't be serious."

"Excuse me, but I don't see a wedding ring on your left hand. You must agree with me somewhat," he pointed out.

But she didn't agree with him. Not at all. "I'm not married because I haven't found the right person yet. But that doesn't mean I think marriage is a snake pit."

"And yet you haven't gotten married."

"I almost did."

Her admission obviously surprised him. "How close is almost?"

Even now, she couldn't believe she'd been so foolish as to trust her ex-fiancé, Don. Everyone had told her Don was a flirt and a player. Her family had told her. Her friends had told her. Heck, even the man catering the reception had told her. But she'd refused to see the truth.

"I was stood up at the altar," she said, then clarified, "well, not actually stood up. Don did show up at the church. We even made it to the altar. But after that, things didn't work out."

Trent scooted closer to her. "Hey, you can't stop there. I'm hooked now. So, tell me what happened. You were standing at the altar with what's-his-name, and then?"

Although Erin rarely discussed her wedding fiasco, it no longer bothered her to talk about it. In fact, she firmly believed things had turned out for the best. Don hadn't been the right man for her. He'd been far too wild and immature to get married.

"When the minister got to the part where he asked Don if he 'took this woman,' Don looked at me, said 'Sorry, babe,' grabbed my maid of honor's hand, and they ran out of the church."

Trent stared at her. "You're kidding, right? He ran off with your maid of honor?"

Erin nodded. "Yes. They even left in the car with Just Married on the back."

Trent let out a long, low whistle. "Wow. That stinks.

So you had no idea he was in love with your maid of honor?"

Erin reached over and idly patted Brutus. "Hadn't a clue."

"Man, I'm sorry. That must have been tough. On behalf of my gender, I apologize."

"Thanks, but it's not necessary. Don and I weren't meant to be together. It's good we didn't go through with the wedding."

She looked at the man sitting next to her. From the way Delia described him, it sounded like Trent was a lot like Don. The handsome chief supposedly didn't date anyone for very long, either.

"There he goes again," Trent said, nodding at Brutus, who was chasing his tail. "He does that all the time. Sometimes he gets going so fast it's hard to tell where one end of him stops and the other starts."

Erin smiled as she watched the puppy play. "He likes to have fun." She couldn't help adding, "From what I hear, so does his owner."

"Ouch." Trent slapped his chest. "Got me with that one."

"You know what I mean." She reached out and patted Brutus, knowing she shouldn't be sitting here talking to Trent. She should tell him to head on home. She had a long day tomorrow and should be in bed by now.

But she was enjoying Trent's company. He was a nice guy, even if he was a flirt. Besides, she'd learned her lesson with Don. Flirts were fine as long as you didn't take them seriously.

And she certainly didn't take Trent Barrett seriously.

"Come on, let me show you a couple of things you can try with Brutus to get him to behave," she offered.

Before she made a move, Trent stood and held out one hand to her. "Allow me."

Without thinking, Erin took his hand and let him pull her up. What she hadn't counted on was the reaction she'd have as soon as her skin touched his. Desire flashed between them, and she couldn't seem to get it through her thick head that touching Trent was a bad thing. In fact, her entire body seemed to find the idea utterly delightful.

Trent also seemed to find the contact between them enticing. Erin could clearly see a healthy dose of male lust in his gaze.

"Tell me what you want me to do," he said.

Oh, now there was a loaded question. Her gaze dropped to his mouth. She could think of several things she'd like him to do.

"You should use positive reinforcement whenever possible," she said, not surprised that her voice sounded breathless and excited. Trent still held her hand, and she did nothing to break the contact.

"Positive reinforcement," he repeated softly. His thumb lightly caressed the back of her hand.

"Um, yes. Whenever he does something you like, praise him," Erin said.

A wicked grin grew on Trent's face, and he moved closer to her.

"Praise seems like a good way to go," he said.

Her gaze was fixed on his lips. She'd bet anything that Trent was a world-class kisser. He probably could make a woman forget everything with only one kiss.

49

Heck, she was having trouble remembering what she was talking about, and he hadn't even kissed her.

"When he does something you like, say 'Good boy' so he'll know to do it again," she said absently, her attention still focused on Trent's mouth and the seductive caress of his thumb on her hand.

Trent slowly leaned forward and lightly brushed his lips across hers.

Oh. My. Erin sighed with pure bliss as tingles ran through her.

"Good boy," she said immediately.

Trent chuckled and kissed her again.

4

While Trent gathered Erin closer and deepened the kiss, he couldn't help thinking that maybe he was the one who needed a couple of behavior lessons. Dang, he hadn't come here tonight intending on kissing Erin, but yet here he was, kissing her like there was no tomorrow.

And having one heck of a good time. Man, Erin could kiss, so he didn't waste a lot of time analyzing the situation. He just accepted his good fortune.

Things were humming right along when the yip-yip-yapping sound of Brutus tugged them both back to reality.

"Let's ignore him," Trent murmured against Erin's soft lips. "Brutus will be fine."

"What if he needs to answer the call of nature?" For a split second, Trent almost said "Who cares." After all, it was the strongest rule of the male species—you didn't interrupt when your friend was kissing a pretty lady. Brutus was male. He should know this stuff.

But leave it to the furball to decide he couldn't wait a couple of minutes to answer that call of nature.

Blasted dog.

"That was a surprise," Erin said as she backed away from him like he was a big old pile of nuclear waste.

Uh-oh. Sounded like she had regrets.

"A nice surprise," Trent said, hoping to salvage the situation.

But he was obviously too late because Erin's expression had taken on a determined cast that he just knew didn't bode well. At least not if he was hoping there'd be more kissing between them anytime in the near future. And he had been hoping for more kissing.

Trent glared down at Brutus, who was once again happily chasing his own tail. Dang furball.

"We shouldn't have done that," Erin said. Although her voice was soft, her tone was firm. The lady meant business. "I'm not interested in a relationship at this particular moment."

Hell, he wasn't interested in a relationship at any particular moment. But if Erin didn't want a relationship, he sure-as-shootin' would bet she really wouldn't be interested in what he had in mind.

"Okay," he said, leaning down and scooping up Brutus.

Erin eyed him closely. "I don't mean to offend you. The kiss was lovely."

She was downright cute. She was giving him the brush-off big time but still concerned about his feelings.

"I'm fine, Erin. No broken heart. No trampled feelings." He took a step closer to her, then added with a grin, "To tell you the honest truth, I don't go in for relationships myself. Short flings, sure, I'm on board with that. We all can use a little fun. But that whole 'till-death-do-us-part' thing gives me the chills."

As he watched, Erin's expression hardened like cement. "I see. It's nice to know what your feelings are on this subject."

For a split second, he considered backpedaling, but then he decided it was best if Erin knew what kind of guy he was from the start. Still, it wouldn't hurt to soften the news a tad.

"Don't get me wrong. I'm not exactly Brutus here when it comes to the ladies, but I'm not the tied-down type, either."

Erin nodded at Brutus. "I sure hope you're not like Brutus, especially since you've agreed to have him neutered."

Talk about giving a man the chills. Yeow. He literally shivered at the thought. "I still haven't figured out a way to tell Brutus about that."

Apparently switching the subject to Brutus and his impending alteration was enough to soften Erin's mood. She stepped over and patted Brutus on the head.

"You're a good boy, and everything's going to be all right," she cooed.

"Just which one of us are you talking to?" Trent teased.

"Go home, Trent Barrett," Erin said with a laugh. "And take your dog with you."

"Yes, ma'am." Trent looked at Brutus. "Looks like we men have worn out our welcome. But I'm pretty sure if we mind our manners, she'll let us come back on Wednesday for more obedience lessons."

"Yes, you can come back on Wednesday," she said. "But next time, I want both of you to behave."

Trent nodded his head and helped Brutus nod, too. "You bet. We boys promise we'll be absolute angels."

Erin sighed and started walking toward the front door again. "Brutus might behave like an angel on Wednesday, but even though I haven't known you long, Trent, I'm positive you haven't got a single angelic bone in your body."

Trent chuckled as he scooted out the front door. "You may have a point."

Erin patted Brutus' head. "You take care of this dumb animal, okay?"

Trent looked at Brutus. "This time, I'm certain she's talking to you."

ERIN TIPPED HER HEAD AND STUDIED THE BUNCH OF flowers sitting on the doorstep to her store. They looked like they'd been yanked out of the ground, not picked gently.

"Nice collection of weeds," Leigh Barrett said as she came to stand next to Erin. "Did you grow them yourself?"

"I think it's a bouquet of flowers left by someone," Erin told the younger woman. "Maybe by the same person who left Pookie here."

Leigh made a loud snorting noise. "First off, those

aren't flowers, they're weeds. Second off—" She pointed down the sidewalk. "They're everywhere. It looks like someone was carrying a bundle and dropped a bunch on the way."

"On the way to putting the bouquet in front of the door to my store?" Erin didn't like this a bit. It was strange. Who would do such a thing?

Leigh put her hands on Erin's shoulders and turned her so she was looking down the sidewalk. "Look at that, Erin. Whoever was carrying those weeds dropped them everywhere. Yeah, you may have the majority in front of your door, but if you think a secret admirer did this, then how do you explain the weeds in front of the Slurp and Burp?"

What in the world was Leigh talking about? "The Slurp and Burp?"

"Roy's Cafe. Great chicken fried steak, by the way. Anywho, as you can see, Roy's got a lot of weeds in front of his door, too. Now what kind of secret admirer do you suppose would leave both you and Roy weeds? Roy's a great guy, but he's in his sixties and married to boot."

Erin felt the panic inside her slowly seep away. Leigh was right. There were flowers, er, weeds, in front of Roy's Cafe, too. This didn't seem to be a deliberate gesture.

"Thanks," she told Leigh, meaning it more than she could explain.

"No problem. But to make you feel a million times better, let's have Trent tell you what I just said in his official chief-of-police voice. Things always sound more impressive when a person in uniform says them. I mean, would you let someone wearing a thong and sunscreen take out your appendix?" She tugged on Erin's arm, and they started down the sidewalk toward the police station. "Well, maybe you would if he looked really hot in that thong, but for the most part, you wouldn't."

Erin blinked. Leigh certainly was full of zest. "I don't need Trent to reassure me." In fact, Trent was the last person she wanted to see right now. She still couldn't believe she'd actually let him kiss her last night. What had she been thinking?

Her own personal code of honesty set off an alarm. She was lying and she knew it. She hadn't let Trent kiss her. Nope. She'd been a very active participant throughout the entire process.

You'd think being jilted at your wedding would teach a woman a thing or two about men. Apparently, all it had taught her was to wrap her arms around Trent's neck when she wanted him to deepen the kiss. The experience sure hadn't taught her anything useful, like how to say, "No, thank you. I'd rather you not kiss me."

But no siree, she hadn't said a thing to stop Trent. She'd fallen right in line with the plan and kissed the man back like a crazy woman.

"I don't want to see Trent," Erin blurted. "Thanks anyway, but I have to open my store."

"Erin, Trent's not going to arrest you," Leigh said, and then she laughed.

Erin didn't like the sound of that laugh one bit. Boy, this young woman was headstrong. She didn't seem to even have the ability to hear the word no. But Erin had been raised in a family of headstrong people, so Leigh didn't intimidate her.

"I do not want to see Trent," Erin said firmly and slowly.

"Why not?"

At the sound of Trent's voice, Erin yelped. Then hoped the ground would open up and swallow her.

She'd yelped? She never yelped. She wasn't the startled, easily scared type.

But there was no denying the obvious—she'd yelped when she'd heard Trent's voice.

Knowing he stood directly behind her, Erin shot a frown at Leigh, who only laughed, then turned to face the man who had starred in her dreams last night.

"Hi," he said. He had a definite twinkle in his deep-blue eyes. "It's nice to see you today."

"Hi," she said, inwardly cringing when the word came out breathless and more than a little flirtatious. Oh, for pity's sake. First, she'd yelped, now she was doing a Marilyn Monroe impersonation? Her hormones were getting way out of control. So he was good-looking. So what? And so he was without a doubt the best kisser she'd ever kissed. Again, so what? None of that excused her behavior. When she got back to the store later, she intended on giving her libido a stern talking-to.

"Since Erin seems to have temporarily lost the ability to speak, I'll tell you why we're here. Erin has weeds in front of her store," Leigh said, looking at Erin for confirmation.

"I thought they might be flowers someone had left for me. Like someone left Pookie and the birdhouse,"

Erin explained, thrilled that her voice finally sounded normal. Or close to it, anyway. Trent was standing right next to her, and she was only human after all.

"Someone left you flowers?" he asked.

"Weeds," Leigh explained once again. "They left her weeds. But there are weeds in front of Roy's, too, and I'm sure no one's trying to woo him."

Trent turned his attention to his sister. "Why exactly are you here?"

"I was going to Precious Pets to buy a new toy for Brutus," she said.

Trent raised one eyebrow. "A toy? The furball's got all the toys he needs. Plus, he's got my living room sofa to chew on, and my shoelaces to play tug-of-war with. Seems to me he's all set."

"Ha, ha." Leigh looked at Erin. "It's hard to believe we're related, isn't it?"

"Um, let me think," Erin managed to say with a moderately straight face.

"I know, we look so much alike, how could you not know we're related," Leigh said.

"Leigh, truthfully, your personalities are similar," Erin admitted.

Not laughing at the offended expressions both Trent and Leigh got was one of the toughest things Erin ever did. She couldn't say offhand which of them looked more upset.

Trent was the first one to speak. "I realize we don't know each other very well, but my personality is nothing like Leigh's."

Leigh bobbed her head. "That's right. Trent's more like Chase, and Nathan's more like...well, he doesn't really fit in with Trent and Chase. Come to think of it, Chase isn't really like Trent because—"

"Stop. Leigh, that's enough. I think we've shared enough family history with poor Erin." Trent leaned closer to his sister and added, "And I'm nothing like Chase."

Leigh snorted and looked at Erin. "See, this is the problem with growing up with three brothers. They drive you nuts, but what can you do? It's not like you can send them back. I mean, come on, what are you going to use for a receipt?"

Okay, now Erin was confused, but at least Leigh had taken her mind off how flustered she was at seeing Trent again. "What?"

Trent draped one arm around Leigh's shoulders. "Let me translate. Leigh thinks I, and her other two brothers Chase and Nathan, meddle too much in her life. But she loves us anyway. Now what about those weeds?"

Erin looked from one Barrett to the other. Wow. There were four of these people? Both Trent and Leigh had personality and zest to spare. Were they all like this? Chase had seemed nice, but she hadn't met the other brother yet.

"The weeds?" Leigh prompted again. "Tell Trent about the weeds."

Like a derailed train, it took Erin a couple of minutes to get back on track. Finally, she said, "I believe they might be flowers. Or at least whoever left them might have thought they were leaving flowers. Can you look at the video?"

Leigh tugged on her brother's arm. "Come on. We'll show you the evidence. You'll see that they're weeds, not flowers, and they've been dropped all along the sidewalk, not left intentionally in front of Erin's store." She gave Erin a sympathetic look. "But don't worry, I'm sure someday you'll meet a nice man who will bring you flowers."

Erin's mouth dropped open. "This isn't about me secretly wanting someone to give me flowers. I'm concerned that someone is leaving things in front of my store."

Thankfully Trent was on her side. "I understand completely. Now let's go take a look at these flowering weeds."

The three of them headed toward Precious Pets, but long before they reached it, Erin realized something was wrong. The flowers were gone. All the ones that had been scattered on the sidewalk were missing. When they got close enough to Precious Pets for her to see, she could tell they were gone from outside her store as well.

"Hey, where'd they go?" Leigh asked, scanning up and down the sidewalk. "Someone stole the weeds." She shook her head. "It's a sorry day when you can't even leave weeds lying around without some bonehead stealing them."

Trent sighed loudly and pointed at a trash can just beyond Precious Pets. "Looks like someone picked them up and tossed them."

Erin walked over to one of the dark-green trash cans the city had placed along each sidewalk in the business district. Sure enough, the flowers had been thrown away. Now, looking at the pile in the trash can, they did look more like weeds than flowers.

When Trent came over to stand next to her, Erin said, "I guess I was overreacting. These are weeds."

"Weeds someone sent to their final resting place in weed heaven," Leigh said as she looked into the trash can. "Oh, well. I'm sure they lived long and happy lives."

This time, Erin was the one to sigh. She headed over and unlocked her store. She'd spent way too much time this morning worrying about these weeds. That whole thing with Pookie and the birdhouse had made her jumpy.

"Thanks for stopping by," Erin said to Trent. Before Trent could answer, Leigh shoved past both of them and walked inside the store. "You two go ahead and talk while I find a toy for Brutus. I'm in a hurry and need to...um, hurry."

With that, Leigh shut the door to Precious Pets in Erin's face.

"You'll have to excuse Leigh," Trent said dryly. "She was raised by a pack of wild, unruly brothers and has the manners of a Barrett boy."

Erin laughed. "She certainly does have her own approach to life."

"Yes, she does." His gaze held hers, and suddenly, Erin relived every single thing that had happened between them last night. The talk. The fun. The kiss.

"This is kind of awkward," she admitted.

He frowned. "What is? I didn't mind stopping by to look at the flowers. But I have to agree with Leigh on this one. I think someone probably dropped them. Maybe they had weeded that planter down by the hardware store and were just carting the weeds up here to the trash can. I'll look at the video, but I doubt it's anything to worry about."

Erin looked at the hardware store that sat kitty-corner across the street from Precious Pets. The planter out front was indeed weed-free. And the trash can near her store was the closest. Trent's theory made a lot of sense.

"I guess you're right. But that isn't what I meant when I said this was awkward." She looked directly at him. "I meant the kiss."

"You guys kissed?"

This muffled question came from inside the store.

Erin spun around and realized Leigh stood in front of the display window right by the front door.

Horrified, she turned back to look at Trent. Rather than being upset, he chuckled. "Well, now that Leigh knows, it won't be long before the whole town does. Don't let it bother you. When folks ask about us kissing—"

"People are going to ask me about it? Why would they care?"

This time, Leigh was the one to laugh from inside the store, but Erin ignored her.

"Seriously, Trent. It was only a kiss. I'm sure no one will care in the slightest," Erin said, but she wasn't sure which of them she was trying to convince.

Obviously herself, since Trent looked like he was struggling to keep from laughing again. "Maybe you're right, Erin. Maybe Leigh won't tell everyone in town that we kissed." He looked over Erin's shoulder, apparently at Leigh, and added, "At least she won't if she knows what's good for her."

Behind her, Erin could hear Leigh muttering, but she couldn't make out what the younger woman was saying. It didn't matter anyway. Even if people in town did hear about the kiss, she couldn't believe they would care. And even if they did care, she could tell them politely that it was none of their business. After all, she and Trent weren't going to get involved. They weren't going to show up around town on dates.

Trent must have read her mind, because he teased, "If anyone asks about us, say in your best cop voice, 'there's nothing to see here, so move along.' That should take care of the problem."

Erin smiled at his nonsense. What was it about Trent Barrett that could make her weak in the knees one second and laughing the next? The man certainly was fun to be around, but Erin had the scarred heart to prove that fun men were the most dangerous kind. They'd break your heart, usually without meaning to, but they'd break it just the same.

"I think I'm going to go inside now," Erin told him, her smile long since gone. "Again, thank you."

Behind her, she heard Leigh ask, "For what? The kiss?" Then Leigh laughed again.

"I don't suppose there's any way you could arrest her, is there?" Erin asked Trent.

Trent scratched his jaw and said, "Man, if I could, I would. Have a nice day."

With that, he headed back toward the police station. Erin watched him go, at least she did until she realized that two ladies outside of Roy's Cafe were checking him out as he walked by. One of them even let out a wolf whistle that made Trent laugh.

Behind her, Erin could hear Leigh sputtering with laughter, too.

What kind of town was this? What made the people here act this way?

And what was she going to do if it was contagious?

5

"Now that's a heartwarming sight, a man and his dog."

Trent was walking Brutus to the Wednesday night dog obedience class and so far, every person he'd met in town had felt obligated to comment on his dog. He glanced up, not a bit surprised to see his brother Nathan was the doofus this time.

"Yeah, well, at least dogs like me," Trent shot back. He smiled at Nathan's fiancée, Emma Montgomery. Emma leaned down and petted Brutus.

"He's a cute dog," she said.

Brutus, sensing praise, launched into a series of flips, hops, yips, and yaps. Way to be dignified.

Hoping to distract his brother from Brutus' behavior, Trent asked, "What brings you two downtown tonight?"

They shared a grin, and Trent's internal antenna went up.

LORI WILDE & LIZ ALVIN

"We're out for a stroll. You know, take in the sights," Nathan said, the grin still lurking around his mouth.

"Dang it all, Nathan, what are you up to? I already have more trouble with Leigh than ten men and a saint could handle. I sure don't need you messing with me."

Nathan laughed. "I said we were out for a stroll. That's all. Ease off, there, Chief."

Trent looked at Emma, hoping that since the woman wasn't part of his lamebrain family yet that she was maintaining some sort of control over the man she intended on marrying. "Is that true, Emma? Are you two simply taking a walk?"

Emma looked from Trent to Nathan then back to Trent. Ah, hell, something really was up.

"We are walking," was all she said.

Trent turned to his brother. "Where? Where are you walking to?"

Nathan's grin grew. "Oh, you know, here and there. Here to the ice cream parlor for a cone. Then maybe later, we'll go there."

Trent gave his brother his meanest, most effective narrowed-eyed look. As usual, Nathan didn't bat an eye. "Where's there, Nathan?"

"Emma and I thought we might stop by Precious Pets to see how your puppy training lessons are going. Leigh says your dog is having some problems keeping up with the rest of the class. Maybe after Emma and I watch for a while, we can give you some pointers. Purely in the interest of helping Brutus, of course."

Trent would rather be dipped in honey and strapped to an ant pile. And he didn't believe for a second that Nathan's interest was in the dog. His brother wanted to meet Erin. No doubt Leigh had been spinning all sorts of tales about the two of them. She'd probably already told most of the town about the kiss.

Great. Just what he needed. An audience. "You're wasting your time, Nathan," he said as he steered Brutus toward Precious Pets. "Erin's helping me with Brutus. There's nothing going on between us, so there's no reason for you to stop by to meet her."

Once again, Emma and Nathan shared a look that spoke volumes. They didn't believe for a second that there wasn't something going on.

"I like to meet new people," Emma said. "Erin sounds like an interesting person."

Trent liked his soon-to-be sister-in-law, but she wasn't a very good liar. The two of them were taking a stroll all right, a stroll right to Erin's shop.

"You're wasting your time," he said. "For starters, Brutus isn't doing that badly, so there's nothing interesting to watch."

"I think I'd like to take a look at the shop," Nathan said. "I'm always interested in new businesses coming to Honey."

Nathan owned Barrett Software, the largest employer in town. Although Trent knew Nathan encouraged and helped other businesses, he also knew his brother's visit this evening had nothing to do with chamber of commerce goodwill and everything to do with the Barrett ornery streak. He and his brothers and sister had a history of butting into each other's lives. Most of the time, he thought it was a good idea. After all, they loved each other enough to care.

But being on the receiving end of that ornery streak was pretty darn annoying.

Trent had reached the outside of Precious Pets. Hoping to get this over with quickly, he shoved open the door and waved at the interior of the store. "This is Precious Pets. That's the owner, Erin. The other people standing there staring at us are the members of Brutus' obedience class. Now you've seen everything there is to see. You might as well head on over to the ice cream shop."

But naturally, it wasn't that easy. Nathan and Emma insisted on going inside to meet Erin. Left with no choice, Trent followed them inside and introduced them to the petite brunette.

Erin shook their hands. "It's really nice to meet both of you. Leigh mentioned your wedding is in a few weeks. You must be busy."

"Yes. But it's wonderful." Emma snuggled against Nathan, who proceeded to get a goofy look on his face.

Trent tried to resist the urge to roll his eyes but failed. At least he did manage to keep his mouth shut, but it wasn't easy.

"We hear you're helping Trent," Nathan said, cutting a devious look in Trent's direction.

Trent frowned at his brother. "Don't you have some-place you need to be?"

A lazy grin crossed Nathan's face. "Nope. I'm all clear. Thanks for thinking of me, though." He turned back to Erin. "I know you're new in town, so Emma and I would love it if you would come to our wedding. You can get Trent to show you where the church is, and the reception is going to be at our house. And if

Trent minds his manners, he can come to the wedding, too."

"Cute, real cute," he said, shooting Nathan a narrow-eyed look.

After first making a mental note to disown Nathan, Trent decided if he couldn't get rid of his meddling brother, then Brutus sure could. With a nudge of his foot, he got Brutus to shift toward Nathan. Spotting shoelaces, Brutus pounced on Nathan's running shoes and set to work gnawing his little heart out.

Good dog.

"Whoa, fella, you've got manners as bad as your old dad." Nathan leaned down and scooped the puppy up. "Looks like you've got your work cut out for you," he said to Erin. "Think you can handle these two, or should we call in some zookeepers for reinforcements?"

"I'll manage," Erin said with a laugh, and Trent would have resented it if the sound of her laughter hadn't been silky and sexy and enticing. He found himself hoping she'd laugh some more because he found it as appealing as Brutus found shoelaces.

"I think Erin has everything under control," Emma said, pulling Trent's attention back to the conversation.

Deciding he was tired of this game, Trent snagged his puppy away from Nathan. "I think y'all have enjoyed yourself enough for one evening. Now excuse us because Brutus and I have a class to attend."

He set Brutus down. "Come on, furball." Then he headed toward the back of the shop to the area where Erin held the lessons. Miracle of miracles, Brutus actually trotted after him for once.

Behind him, he heard his brother laugh, but shoot,

he didn't care. Just because Nathan had gone sappy and fallen in love didn't give him the right to go meddling in other people's lives. And Chase and Leigh were just as bad. Yeah, Erin was cute. And smart. And funny. That didn't mean he was going to fall in love with her. Heck, he wasn't going to fall in love with anyone. Like it or not, his family needed to jettison their plan and soon. Because if this kept up, he was going to find himself a new family.

And next time, he'd pick one that wasn't insane.

"Wow, you certainly have a sweet tooth. If I ate that much candy, I'd get so big, I'd form my own gravitational pull. You must have one heck of a metabolism."

Erin recognized the voice immediately. Turning, she found Leigh Barrett standing behind her in line. "Hi, Leigh. How are you?"

Leigh grinned. "Great. So what's up with all the candy?"

Erin wasn't sure what they were talking about, which was a fairly common situation for her since coming to Honey. "Candy?"

The younger woman pointed at Erin's grocery cart. "You've got quite a selection there."

What in the world was she—

Erin glanced at her cart, then stared in stunned silence at the contents. Leigh hadn't been kidding. Seven or eight bags of chocolate candy sat on the top.

Erin scooted the candy aside to see if this really was

her cart. Maybe she'd grabbed the wrong one. She'd stopped for a couple of minutes to talk to Delia, then she'd come right here to the checkout line. Maybe she'd gotten mixed up when she'd returned to her cart.

A quick glance at the other contents proved that she hadn't. This was her cart, but someone had put several bags of candy in it.

How weird.

"My favorites are the ones with caramel centers. But I like the peanut butter ones, too." Leigh leaned past Erin and said, "Ooooh, I like those nut clusters as well. Are you in a major funk and that's why you're buying so much chocolate? I always eat chocolate when I'm down."

Erin pulled her attention away from the contents of her cart and looked at Leigh. "You get depressed? When? It doesn't seem possible."

Leigh laughed. "You're right. I don't get down too often. I'm an upbeat person by nature."

Upbeat. Offbeat. Both described Leigh. "I don't tend to get down too often, either," Erin said.

"So what's with all the chocolate, then?"

That's what Erin was trying to figure out. "I didn't put this candy in my cart," she said, lifting it out. "I think someone else did."

Erin surveyed the store. No one was watching her, but she couldn't help wondering if the candy had been deliberately put in her cart. Was this another little gift like Pookie, the birdhouse, and the flowers? Or was she simply letting her imagination run away with her?

She honestly didn't know.

She looked down at the candy. Maybe this was

another of those instances. In fact, the more she thought about it, the more doubtful it seemed that someone had done this deliberately. For starters, the store was crowded, so mixing up carts would be easy. It had to be an innocent mistake.

Didn't it?

"Don't worry about the candy. Just set it here on the side. They'll put it back on the shelf."

"Thanks." Erin set the candy aside, still puzzled. "It just seems odd."

"I wouldn't think anything of it. This sort of thing happens to me all the time," Leigh said. "I once found a pregnancy test kit in my cart. The cashier was a friend from high school, and she noticed the box before I did. She told the carryout, who told the store manager, and before I could say 'are you out of your mind?' the whole store knew. Thankfully, Elsie VanDerHauffen was still in the store and quickly explained that the kit was hers." Leigh rolled her eyes. "Boy, did that cause a stir because Elsie's husband was away working on an oil rig in the Gulf and hadn't been home in eleven months. I mean, come on, how could she be pregnant, right?"

Leigh paused, and Erin stared at her. What in the world was she talking about? But since Leigh seemed to expect some sort of response, the best Erin could manage was, "Huh?"

With a laugh, Leigh continued. "Lost you there, didn't I? Anyway, turns out Elsie and Bemie, that's her husband, had gone on a second honeymoon at some motel near Galveston, and she hadn't breathed a word to anyone. But now everyone knew. So, you see my point."

"Not even remotely," Erin admitted.

"Someone put the candy in your cart by mistake," Leigh said. "Just like Elsie put her stuff in my cart by mistake. Just consider yourself lucky you won't have to worry about three brothers having simultaneous strokes like I had to. For a second there when I couldn't convince anyone the pregnancy test kit wasn't mine, well, let's just say things looked bleak. All you have is a few bags of candy. No one's going to start any rumors about you. Well, not exciting ones. Having a sweet tooth is nothing compared to having a surprise baby, so consider yourself lucky."

When Leigh put it like that, Erin had to admit the candy didn't seem suspicious at all. "I'm sure that's what happened. Someone put it there by mistake."

After putting the rest of her groceries on the counter, she told Leigh, "For a second there, I thought someone might have put the candy in my cart deliberately."

Leigh frowned. "Now why would someone want to make you fat?" Suddenly, her expression brightened. "You mean this could be some sort of revenge thing. Wow. Wouldn't that be something? Nothing exciting ever happens in Honey, and boy, don't I know it. Most days this town is about as exciting as watching dirt age. Maybe you'll bring some excitement to this town. First, there was Pookie. Then the birdhouse. And finally, the weeds thing—but to tell you the truth, I'm still not sure that meant anything. And now the candy." She grinned. "You haven't stolen anyone's husband lately by any chance? Maybe someone's trying to get back at you."

"Of course I haven't." Erin drew a deep, calming

breath into her lungs when Leigh looked disappointed. There was no way that Erin believed for a second that any town in which the Barrett family lived would be boring. "I just thought the candy might be—"

"A present from a secret admirer." Leigh studied the bags of candy Erin had set aside. "They could be, I guess. But knowing how boring this place is, I think a mix-up is the more likely scenario. Still, you should tell Trent."

Yes, telling Trent sounded like the most reasonable thing to do. And ever since Nathan and Emma had stopped by the store over a week ago, Trent had been a complete gentleman in class. Well, at least as much of a gentleman as a man like Trent could be. He still had that rogue's gleam in his eyes whenever he looked at her, but he'd kept his hands and his lips to himself.

For Trent, that was excellent behavior.

"I think I'll stop by the station on my way home and talk this over with Trent," Erin told Leigh. "Just to let him know."

"Sounds good. But Trent isn't at the station. He's already left for the day. Why don't you swing by his house and tell him?"

"I couldn't simply drop by. That would be rude." More than that, she might end up interrupting something like a dinner party or worse, a date. "I'll stop by his office tomorrow or the next day and tell him."

Leigh seemed perplexed by Erin's answer. "Why would stopping by his house be rude? This is Honey. People stop by to say hi all the time." She opened her gargantuan purse and started digging through it. "Hold on a sec."

Erin hadn't a clue why, but Leigh seemed so deep in thought that she hated to interrupt her. Still, once the other young woman finally found whatever it was she was searching for, Erin intended on explaining that even though the residents of Honey might drop in on each other unannounced all the time, it wasn't the sort of thing she was used to doing. Having grown up in a family with three sisters, she valued her privacy and figured other people valued theirs as well.

Even people who lived in Honey.

With a flourish, Leigh yanked her cell phone out of her purse, and before Erin could do much to protest, she called Trent.

"Heads-up. Erin's on her way over to your house," Leigh said. Then she hung up. "There you go. All set."

Erin barely managed to keep her mouth from falling open. At no point in the brief conversation were the words "can Erin stop by" or "would you mind" used.

Flat-out amazed by the other woman's approach, Erin pointed out, "You didn't ask him if I could come over. You told him. What if he'd rather I not stop by?"

"Why wouldn't he want you to stop by? No offense, Erin, but you're thinking way too much about this. Folks around here expect people to stop by at all times; otherwise, they wouldn't live in Honey. They'd live someplace like Dallas or Houston where people only come over when invited."

Leigh said the last sentence with so much distaste in her voice that Erin clearly understood that impromptu visits were considered a definite perk to small-town living. At least they were to Trent's sister. Always a firm believer in fitting in with the natives, Erin made a mental note to not be surprised if people started showing up unannounced on her doorstep.

And as far as going to Trent's house went, well, he had been informed, so her visit would no longer be a surprise. "I guess I can stop by for a couple of minutes," Erin relented. "I'm sure he won't mind."

"Of course he won't," Leigh said, bobbing her head. "And if he's got a girl or two over there, you tell them to take a hike. You're there on official business, so they can chase after him some other time."

Erin froze. Surely Leigh was kidding. But from the look on the young woman's face, she realized Leigh was serious. She honestly thought Erin might run into young women at Trent's house.

Maybe going to see him wasn't such a good idea after all. "On second thought, why don't I just call Trent when I get home? I can tell him everything over the phone."

"Have you always been so timid about things?" Leigh asked.

Timid? No one had ever called Erin timid in her entire life. "Just because I don't want to interrupt his evening doesn't mean I'm timid."

"If you say so," Leigh said with a shrug. "It sure seems timid to me. Maybe you could go through some sort of self-help thing with twelve steps and get over your timidness."

That got to Erin. She wasn't timid. Never had been. And especially now, since starting her new life, she'd made a point of being brave and independent. So what if Trent had someone over at his house? Did that mean she couldn't stop by and tell him what had happened?

"I am not timid," Erin said firmly to Leigh.

"Okeydokey," Leigh said. "So you're going over to Trent's house, then?"

"You bet I am," Erin said.

"Good for you." Leigh's smile turned downright smug. "You have a nice time."

Suspicion trickled over Erin. There was something about Leigh's smile that made her more than a little uncomfortable.

"I'm only going over there to tell him about the candy," Erin felt compelled to say. "There's nothing to smile about."

Leigh's smile only grew wider. "Of course that's why you're going. I'm only smiling because I'm happy that Trent will know what's going on."

Yeah, well, if Trent knew what was going on in this town, then Erin sure hoped he'd tell her. Because frankly, she hadn't a clue.

❧

TRENT OPENED HIS FRONT DOOR AND SMILED. NOW this was a pleasant surprise—Erin on his doorstep.

"Hi," she said. Then before he could say a word, she hurried on. "I hope I haven't disturbed you, but Leigh said I should stop by. Actually, it was more like Leigh insisted I stop by." She peered beyond him to the inside of the house. Since Brutus was yapping at their feet, he couldn't help wondering what she was looking for.

With a glance over his shoulder, he asked, "Is something sneaking up behind me? 'Cause if it is, I'd appreciate a little warning."

When Erin looked at him, she frowned. "What? Oh, no. I was just making sure I wasn't interrupting anything."

Trent chuckled. "Well, I did have a bunch of naked dancing girls over, but when Leigh called, I decided I best send them on home. Figured you'd disapprove. Of course, I can't promise you that Brutus doesn't have a lady friend over. The guy's a real animal."

Erin gave him a wan smile, so Trent knew immediately that something was up.

"You're not disturbing me. What's going on?" He pushed his front door open. Brutus scampered over and did his best to escape before Trent picked him up.

"Nothing, I guess," she said.

But when Erin only gave the pup a halfhearted pat, Trent knew she was lying.

"Come on. Fess up. As much as I'd like to think you stopped by because you were drawn by my sheer charm, I know that isn't the case. So what happened?" he asked.

"Nothing, really." When he continued to give her a dubious look, she added, "It's just that I found some candy in my cart at the grocery store."

"And?"

She blew out a breath of disgust. "I didn't put it there. I can't help thinking it has something to do with Pookie, the birdhouse, and the flowers."

Trent nodded. She might be right. Or it could simply be a mix-up. But either way, Erin was upset, and it seemed like the best idea was to spend some time talking this over with her.

"What did you buy at the grocery store?" he asked.

She frowned, but she still answered him. "I picked up a few things for dinner. Why? Are you thinking that my cart looked like someone else's and that it's all a case of mistaken cart identity?"

"Yeah, sure. Plus, I was wondering if you had anything in your grocery bags we might cook up for dinner. I'm starving."

For a priceless minute, Erin simply stared at him. Then she asked slowly, "You're inviting me to dinner if I supply the food?"

"Hey, I'll cook. Unless, of course, you bought liver. Then I withdraw the offer." He gave a mock shudder. "I can't stand liver."

"I bought the ingredients for spaghetti," she said flatly.

Trent grinned and tugged at her arm. "Good, then by all means, stay for dinner. I'll cook, and you tell me more about what happened at the store."

He could tell Erin was torn. She obviously didn't know what to say, so Trent played his trump card. "Please stay. Look at Brutus' sad face. He wants you to stay. He's so upset at the mere thought that you might leave."

His argument would have carried more weight if Brutus hadn't been panting and looking about as happy as a puppy could be.

Finally, Erin shrugged. "Fine. I'll stay. But I want it on the record that I think you're as devious as your sister."

He nodded. "Duly noted. Now where are those groceries?"

Before she could argue, he headed toward her car to

grab the food. She might think he was devious, but he really did want to talk over what had happened. And sure, he'd like to spend some time with Erin as well. Dinner seemed like the natural solution.

And after all, a guy had to grab every opportunity that came his way.

❧ 6 ❧

Trent took a great deal of satisfaction watching Erin be amazed by his culinary skill. Why was it that women thought men knew everything about cars and nothing about cooking? Well, he was one rancher's son who knew his way around a kitchen.

And he didn't mind showing off for a pretty lady.

"Tada," he said when he set the bowl of perfectly cooked pasta next to the savory sauce he'd created from the ingredients she'd bought and a few of his own thrown in.

"I'm really impressed," Erin said, and he chuckled at her surprised tone.

"Did you honestly think I couldn't cook?" he asked, sitting after she had.

"No. Yes. I guess I didn't picture you as the domestic type."

He handed the bowl of pasta to her and waited while she served herself. "Oh, I'm not domestic. Not in the sense a lot of people mean it. But I can cook. And I clean my own house. Doesn't mean I'm the type to start picking out china patterns, but I can tend to myself."

Erin laughed, and Trent had to admit, he surely loved that sound.

"Calm down," she said. "I wasn't asking you to marry me. I just meant that it's nice when people surprise you with talents you hadn't yet discovered they have."

Okay, now there was no way as a self-respecting male that he could let that comment go without a response.

"I have a lot of talents you haven't discovered yet."

This time when Erin laughed, he was less than enchanted. Especially when she said, "I can't believe you used a line on me."

"Hey, it's not a line," he told her, knowing full well it was a line and not a very good one. But he wasn't about to admit that to her.

She was still laughing when she countered, "Oh, yes, it most certainly was a line. You were intimating some-thing, probably something like what you said in class a couple of weeks ago."

A light flush colored her face, and Trent leaned forward. "Gee, Erin, I have no idea what you're talking about. What line in class?"

He expected her to get flustered or glance away, but she didn't. Instead, she stopped laughing and looked him dead in the eye as she said, "You know exactly what I'm talking about."

He pretended to consider what she'd said. "I'm racking my brain here, and I still don't remember a thing," he teased.

"Liar," she said softly.

"For the record, that definitely wasn't a line. And also, you were the one who started it with all that talk about consistency and firmness." He took a long sip of iced tea before he added, "I was being a perfect gentleman at the time."

"To quote your sister—" she said, then she snorted.

Laughter burst out of Trent, and Erin laughed, too. Brutus joined in, yapping and chasing his own tail. By the time Trent finally got himself under control, he realized he hadn't laughed that much in a long, long time.

For a second, they sat looking at each other, humor still in their gazes. But along with the humor was attraction. Strong, vibrant attraction that made Trent want to kiss her again.

"Do you want more?" she asked.

Oh, yeah, did he ever.

He could picture it now. He'd give her a grin, then circle around to her side of the table, take her in his arms, pull her soft, warm body close and—

"No!"

Trent froze. "Excuse me?"

Thankfully, Erin indicated Brutus. "He's thinking about making a move."

Yeah, well, Brutus wasn't the only guy in the room thinking along those lines. The idea had a lot of appeal to Trent as well.

With effort, he reined in his libido and asked, "What's the furball up to now?"

"He's definitely eyeing your shoelaces. I swear, I'm starting to worry about Brutus. He seems to have a one-track mind."

Trent knew exactly how the puppy felt. Whenever

he was around Erin, he seemed to have a one-track mind as well. He gave the pup a stern look. Sure enough, Brutus was slowly creeping toward Trent's feet.

"Furball, what is it with you and shoelaces? Do you need more roughage in your diet?"

"He likes being around you," Erin said. "Dogs are pack animals. You're part of his pack."

"And chewing on my shoelaces would be a sign of what?"

"He wants to play with you."

"After dinner. Right now, I'm playing with you." As soon as the words left Trent's mouth, he knew what Erin's response would be. She didn't disappoint him, either. She immediately frowned.

"There you go with the pickup lines again," she said, then turned her attention back to her dinner.

"That's not a pickup line," he protested. "A double entendre, maybe. But not a line. You've got it all confused. A line is something like 'Hey baby, Heaven's missing an angel since you're here on Earth.'"

She crinkled her nose. "Yuck. Tell me you've never said anything so lame before. No woman would ever fall for something that dumb."

Trent decided not to enlighten Erin and risk ending up with a plateful of spaghetti in his lap. He hated to admit it, but he'd used that line and several like it before with great results.

"Okay, that's a bad example," he admitted. "A good line doesn't sound a thing like a line."

For a few minutes, they ate in silence. Trent knew Erin was dying to ask him what a good line was, but he also could tell she was trying her hardest not to ask.

Finally, she dropped her fork on her plate and looked at him.

"Okay, I can't stand it. Give me an example of a good line."

Trent barely refrained from smiling. Instead, he shook his head. "A good line is no line at all. It's taking the time to really understand the lady you're interested in and being honest with her." He leaned forward a little, then said, "For instance, do you know you have the most amazing laugh? I love the way it sounds. So free. So wild. I've never met anyone who laughs as great as you do."

Erin stared at him, her brown eyes filled with doubt. She didn't know if what he'd just told her was a line he'd used a million times before or the truth. With any other woman, he'd flash a grin and assure her that he was telling the honest truth.

But the funny thing was, this time, he really was telling the truth. He loved the way Erin laughed. And he needed her to know it wasn't a line.

The problem became how to convince her. He knew Erin thought he was a player. Heck, he was. He made no secret of the fact that he liked his single lifestyle.

"I mean it," he said. "You have a great laugh."

Erin rolled her eyes. "You proved your point. The best lines don't sound like lines at all."

"I guess there's no way for me to convince you that wasn't a line, is there?"

She pretended to consider his question, then said, "Nope."

"Okay. So then, why don't you tell me what happened at the grocery store? If I can't convince you of my sincerity, maybe I can impress you with my razor-sharp deductive abilities."

Erin quickly explained what had happened at the store. When she finished, Trent wasn't sure what to make of the candy. More than likely, it had been a mix-up.

"Don't you think it's odd that all of these things keep happening? The flowers, okay, maybe Leigh was right. Maybe they'd been dropped by accident. And sure, maybe the candy was an accident, too." She shrugged. "It just strikes me as an awful lot of accidents."

"Strikes me that way, too." He took another sip of his iced tea and considered her. "Sadly, the video from the weeds/flowers wasn't helpful. Someone did weed the flowerbox across the street from your store, but it was early morning and still dark. I couldn't see who it was. I asked around, and everyone I talked to had no idea what I meant. It was a kind of short person wearing a hoodie. That's all I could make out. It looked like when they finished pulling the weeds, they headed across the street, probably to the trash can. On the way, they dropped lots of the weeds, mostly in front of your store."

Erin was frowning at him. "Did it look like it was on purpose?"

"Hard to tell. Anything else odd happen lately?"

"You mean besides you asking me to stay for dinner so you could use up all of my groceries?"

He chuckled. "Yeah, besides that."

"No. And when I stop to think about it all, it seems silly to be upset." She ran one finger up and down the side of her glass. "It was only a few bags of candy in my cart."

"Still, I'll look into it. A person can't be too careful."

Erin nodded, and then her glance met his. For a second, the attraction level between them zoomed.

Then she said, "You're absolutely right. A person can't be too careful...about a lot of things."

ERIN TIPPED HER HEAD AND STUDIED BRUTUS. "I think he's getting worse rather than better."

Trent nodded. "Yeah, I think so, too. But dang if I can figure out why. I keep doing everything you've shown us in class. But each day, the boy seems to get rowdier."

"He definitely fits into your family," she couldn't resist saying.

Rather than being offended, Trent laughed. "He does at that, doesn't he?"

He scooped up the puppy. "At least, he's definitely related to Leigh. Furball here no more finishes making one mess before he's off making another. Keeps a man busy."

Erin smiled, watching Trent hold Brutus at eye level. No matter what the sexy chief of police said, Erin could tell he really liked the puppy. The two males were cute to watch together, although Erin would prefer it if Brutus took to the lessons a little better.

"Since he just ate, I'm going to take your advice and let him run in the backyard for a bit," Trent said.

"That's a good idea since you're trying to train him."

"Trying is the operative word in that sentence." He glanced at the clock. "Can you stick around for a while longer? I have to go stand outside with Brutus or else he won't take care of business."

That seemed odd. "Why on earth not?"

Trent gave her a rueful grin. "He's afraid of the neighbor's cat. Fluffy scares the bejeepers out of him."

Erin laughed. "This I've got to see. Mind if I come with you two?"

With a wave toward the back door, Trent let her precede him outside. Sure enough, as soon as they got out, Trent had to shoo a cat away before Brutus would step off the patio.

"Yep. That's my dog. Afraid of a cat," Trent said dryly.

"In Brutus' defense, it is a big cat, and he's a small dog."

Trent snorted. "He's also not too keen on spiders, and yesterday he ran back inside after encountering a cricket. Face it, my dog is a coward."

"He's still a puppy. Give him a chance. Besides, Brutus is more of a lover than a fighter."

"Is that a fact? Well, since you're making me get the boy fixed, he won't be a lover for much longer."

"He'll still be sweet and cuddly."

Trent groaned. "Great. I'm going to have a cuddly dog. Just what every chief of police needs. Maybe I should stock up on pink bows in case he feels like dressing up."

Erin laughed. "You are so predictable."

"Why?"

"Why? Look at you. You're taking this personally

that your dog isn't some man-eating killer." She couldn't help adding, "You know, women like guys who aren't he-men all the time. It's nice to show a softer side of your personality now and then."

Trent turned to face her, and he had pure mischief in his eyes. "Oh, really? Is that all women?"

Oops. She should have thought that comment through before she'd made it. Now he was giving her one of his bona fide sure-to-melt-the-toughest-heart looks.

Her gaze drifted to his lips. Just like that. Wham. She was staring at his lips like she had no self-control at all.

Now this was why she shouldn't have stayed for dinner. Sure, visiting with Trent and Brutus had been a lot of fun. And talking to Trent had made her worries about the cart mix-up fade. She now was convinced it had been an accident.

But being around Trent hadn't done a thing to squash the out-of-control attraction she felt toward him. Nope. That was still thriving. Big time. In fact, the attraction factor had gotten a whole lot worse while she'd been here. Not only had he cooked a great dinner for them, but he'd also been a wonderful host.

Now how was she supposed to resist a man who insisted on being terrific? It simply wasn't fair.

He took a deliberate step closer to her. "So are you one of those women who likes men to have a softer side?"

"I was speaking in general terms," she said, although her words would have carried more weight if they hadn't come out all breathless and husky. "I didn't mean me."

"So you just like tough he-man types, then?"

"No."

He chuckled, the sound deep and masculine. "I'm confused, Erin. You don't like strong Alpha guys. You don't like tender Beta guys. What else is left?"

"No guys." When he raised one eyebrow, she hurriedly added, "I mean, I like men. I'm just not interested in men at the moment."

"Ah." He glanced over at Brutus, who was happily chasing his tail, then looked back at her. "That whole 'left at the altar thing,' right?"

"Yes."

He nodded, then slowly smiled. "Tell me, when you are interested in men, which kind do you prefer?"

They were on dangerous ground, and she knew it. Flirting with Trent wasn't smart, but she didn't seem to be able to stop herself. The man had charm to spare.

"I'm not sure. I don't think I have a preference," she said, her gaze tangled up with his.

"Sure you do. Alpha guys are way different from Beta guys. They talk differently. Act differently." His gaze dropped to her lips. "Kiss differently."

Uh-oh. Danger. Warning. Erin sternly told herself to tell Trent this conversation was over. She needed to head home and was through flirting with him.

Unfortunately, even though that was what she told herself to say, what she actually said was, "They do?"

He nodded. "Oh, yeah." Before she could react, he slipped his arms around her waist. "Alpha guys just go for it. Like this."

Even though she was braced for the kiss, she was in no way prepared for it. Because this was one heck of a kiss. Firm, thorough, and completely devastating. Erin quickly found herself slipping her arms around Trent's neck and kissing him back.

When he finally shifted his lips away from hers, she barely resisted the impulse to protest.

"Now see a Beta guy wouldn't act like that," he said, and Erin was thrilled to note his voice was raspy with desire.

"He wouldn't?"

"No. He'd ask first. Something like, 'mind if I kiss you?'"

"Not at all," she said, even though his question hadn't truly been directed to her. But Trent didn't quibble. Instead, he kissed her. Slowly. Gently. Tenderly.

It was every bit as amazing as the first kiss had been, and once again, Erin slipped her arms around his neck and kissed him back.

This time, when he ended the kiss, they were both breathless. He leaned his forehead against hers.

"So which did you like better?" he asked.

She no more could choose than she could say which leg she liked better. And speaking of legs, both of hers were more than a little wobbly at the moment.

"They were both..." Amazing. Wonderful. Arousing. She cleared her throat. "Fine."

He chuckled again, obviously knowing she was lying. But he didn't call her on the lie. Instead, he said, "Glad you liked them."

Then before she could muster even a faint argument about how they shouldn't have kissed at all, Trent dropped his arms and stepped back.

He whistled, and Brutus slowly trotted over to join them. "Guess it's getting late."

"It is?" She blinked, mentally shook herself, then said firmly, "It is. I need to head home." She took a couple of steps toward the house, then reality forced her to turn to face him. "I guess we should talk about those kisses."

"Decided which one you liked best?" He grinned. "Personally, I thought they both had their own advantages."

"That's not what I mean," she said. "I mean we should talk about why we shouldn't have kissed at all, not which kiss was the best."

"Oh, that. Yeah, well, since our kissing this time was simply a research project, I wouldn't worry about it. There was nothing personal involved."

He was so full of hooey Erin didn't know how he could stand himself. But then, his plan of calling the kisses a research project offered her the perfect out. They could skip the whole "you shouldn't have kissed me" thing and go on with their lives.

Worked for her.

"Fine. I guess I'll see you tomorrow night at Brutus' lesson."

He nodded. "You bet."

Figuring there wasn't a thing left to say, she opened the back door and was all set to go inside to get her purse when Trent said, "Hey, Erin."

She stopped but didn't look at him. "Yes?"

"Whoever said research is tedious never met you."

Erin laughed and kept on walking. The sooner she put some distance between herself and Trent Barrett, the better. She was not going to fall for that flirt no matter what he did.

※

TRENT GLANCED AROUND THE WEDNESDAY NIGHT dog obedience class. Man, these pups had come a long way. Almost all of them were sitting nicely in front of their owners, patiently waiting for the class to begin. Even Delia's dog, who was one of Brutus' sisters, was acting like an absolute angel for the older woman and her grandson.

All the dogs were well behaved. Except Brutus. As usual, he was flopped half on one of Trent's shoes, chomping away at the laces.

Dang furball. For the record, he was not Trent's best friend.

"Cut it out," Trent growled at the dog, nudging him with his foot. Brutus wagged his tail and went back to chewing.

"Good behavior is about a lot more than knowing what to do when," Erin told the class as she walked by each dog and rewarded them with a pat on the head. "Good behavior is also about withstanding temptation."

She stopped in front of Brutus, and Trent couldn't help smiling. Yeah, neither he nor his dog seemed any good at withstanding temptation. Brutus couldn't give up chewing shoelaces, and he couldn't give up kissing Erin.

"Brutus, no," Erin said in a firm, no-nonsense voice. "Sit and be still."

To Trent's amazement, Brutus did what she asked. He stopped chewing on the shoelace and sat.

"Well, I'll be," Trent said, and then without thinking, he let out a whistle.

Pandemonium broke out. All of the dogs responded to the whistle by yapping and yipping and chasing each other. Erin shot him a look of pure frustration before clapping her hands and saying, "Sit."

All the puppies settled down. Except for Brutus, who once more returned to eating Trent's shoelaces.

"Guess it was a short-lived victory," Trent said.

"You shouldn't whistle when you're in dog school," Delia's nine-year-old grandson, Zach, said in that stern tone kids loved to use when correcting an adult. "Whistling makes the dogs go crazy."

Trent winked at the kid. "Thanks for the tip."

After first frowning at Trent, Erin smiled at Zach. "You're right. Whistling does get the dogs riled up. I'm sure Chief Barrett won't do it again."

Zach beamed at her compliment, and Trent bit back a chuckle. Fine, the kid was right, and he was wrong. He was man enough to own up to his mistakes, even if they were dumb ones.

"Yeah, I've learned my lesson. No more whistling in class."

This time, he was the one rewarded with one of Erin's smiles. Man, it felt like a punch to the solar plexus. As soon as she smiled at him, the air seemed to whoosh from his lungs, and he found himself unable to look away. She must have felt the same wallop of attraction because she simply stood still, looking at him.

The memory of the kisses they'd shared the night

before burned between them. Both kisses had been amazing. Trent couldn't ever remember kissing a woman who got his blood as fired up as Erin did. Moreover, not only did he have the major hots for her, but he liked her. She was a blast to talk to, lots of fun to share a joke with, and a good sport when it came to taking guff from his family.

Yep, Erin Weber was one special lady.

"So is class over? Can we leave?"

The question came from Delia and made Erin blink and look away from Trent.

"The class?" She blinked again. "Oh, no. Class isn't over. Not at all. As I mentioned before, tonight we're going to work with training your dogs to resist temptation. Your puppies will see a lot of things in life that they'll want but cannot have. You need to train them to bypass the things that are bad for them."

"For instance?" Zach asked.

Erin glanced at Trent, and he knew without a doubt she'd just put him in the category of things she wanted but shouldn't have. Hey, how fair was that? He wasn't a bad guy. He worked a regular job. Knew how to make spaghetti. Why couldn't she have him if she wanted to?

Someone needed to have a talk with her.

Almost as if she heard him, she frowned and looked away from him. "Things that puppies need to resist are eating bugs, chasing cars, chewing on shoes."

Trent glanced down. Sure enough, the furball was happily slobbering all over his shoelaces.

"Okay, so how do you teach temptation resistance? It's difficult not to give in to the things you want." Trent waited until Erin looked at him, then he added, "And sometimes, things that may seem bad aren't at all. Sometimes they're good. Very, very good."

A light flush colored Erin's face as she stared at him. He knew she completely understood what he was talking about.

"Sometimes things that seem good turn out to be very, very bad," she countered slowly, her words heavy with meaning.

"Sometimes you don't know what's good or bad until you try it." Trent knew the entire class was baffled by their conversation, but he couldn't help using this chance to try to change her mind. Erin couldn't simply blow him off when she had a room full of students. And he was absolutely certain that was what she intended on doing. She intended on telling him that the kisses shouldn't have happened and that they were all wrong for each other.

His way of looking at the situation was a lot simpler —what was the harm in having a little fun? They were adults. No one would get hurt. Why make this complicated?

More importantly, why not give in to temptation?

Erin obviously didn't share his sentiment. She took a step closer to him and said slowly, "I don't need to get hit by a freight train to know it would hurt. Therefore, I avoid things I know are dangerous for me."

"So we also need to teach our dogs to avoid trains, right?" Delia asked. "I think that's a good idea. The train comes fairly close to my house, and I couldn't stand for a tragedy to happen."

"Yes." Erin's gaze never moved from Trent. "Definitely avoid trains. And anything else that might cause serious harm. Better safe than sorry is a great motto to live by."

"But a very boring way to live," Trent couldn't help pointing out. "Very, very boring."

"But a whole lot less messy," Erin countered.

He chuckled. "Yeah, but messy done right can be a whole lot of fun."

❧ 7 ❧

Erin smiled at Delia as she and her grandson said goodnight. They were the last to leave following the lesson. Well, almost the last. Trent and Brutus had stayed behind, which didn't surprise Erin. She and Trent needed to talk, not only about the kisses last night, but also his "a mess done right can be fun" attitude.

As soon as she shut the door to the shop, she turned to face him. "I don't agree with your opinion when it comes to messes."

He tipped his head. "Sure? I think the two of us messing around would be a lot of fun."

"Very cute." She started to walk closer to him, and then thought better of the idea. Every time she got too close to Trent, she ended up in his arms. So in an attempt to resist temptation, she decided to keep the distance of the room between them.

Seeing no reason not to be honest, she said, "I don't want to end up hurt."

"Then I'm the perfect guy for you. No one gets hurt in my love life 'cause no one takes it seriously. Life's short, Erin. Why not let yourself have a little fun?" He took a couple of steps closer, so Erin moved back two steps.

"I'm not sure I can have a relationship where—"

He held up both hands. "Whoa. See that's your first mistake. It wouldn't be a relationship. I don't do relationships. I was talking about dating."

"Dating?" Had she really misunderstood his intentions that much? "Oh. I thought you were interested in..." She shrugged, feeling very self-conscious. "Other things than dating."

He chuckled, and once again took two steps forward. Again, she took two steps back. Actually, one and a half because she bumped into the front door. Still, she was far away from him.

"Erin, hon, if the dating goes well, then those other things happen, too. But no one gets all weepy and clingy. And no one leaves the other one standing in front of the altar holding a broken heart." He grinned and looked like the perfect picture of a lady-killer. "See how much nicer my way is? No promises. No heartaches. Clean. Simple."

The most ridiculous thing suddenly happened to Erin. She agreed with Trent. To her complete and absolute amazement, she saw his point. She didn't want to date a man who made her promises, ones she'd take seriously. Her heart was still healing and needed more time.

In which case, Trent really was the right guy for her at this point in her life.

What a wonderful discovery.

"I agree," she said, returning his grin. "I can't believe it, but you're right. If I don't want a man who will break my heart, then you're perfect for me. You keep your dealings with women strictly on a shallow level. There's no love involved. No emotion."

"I don't know if I'd call it shallow so much as uncomplicated. If you dated me, you'd know from the get-go that we weren't heading to the chapel. That way you wouldn't get all wrapped up in the why-isn't-he-calling-me syndrome. My way is simple. We'd date for however long the two of us agreed it was fun, then we'd say adios and still remain friends."

Erin felt like laughing. She couldn't believe she was actually contemplating having a no-strings relationship —oops, make that a non-relationship—with Trent. But she couldn't see the downside. They were both incredibly attracted to each other, while at the same time, they had absolutely no intention of spending the rest of their lives together. No strings definitely seemed the way to go.

"Sounds good to me," Erin said.

This time when he took two deliberate steps forward, so did she. Grinning at each other, they each took two more steps closer. Finally, they took two more, and ended up standing toe-to-toe.

"Why, Ms. Weber, I'm so glad I bumped into you," he said in that deep, silky voice she loved so much. "I've been wanting to ask you to dinner. Are you free tomorrow night?"

Anticipation hummed through Erin's veins. "We could consider the dinner we shared last night to be our first date," she pointed out.

His grin turned wicked. "I'm shocked. Here I thought you were the shy, retiring type when all along, you've been plotting to take advantage of me."

His silliness made her smile as she slipped her arms around his shoulders. "Do you mind?"

"Not one bit," he said. "You take advantage of me whenever you want."

"Good. Because now seems like the perfect time."

Trent must have agreed because he leaned down and kissed her.

❧

TRENT HADN'T EXPECTED ERIN TO COME AROUND TO his way of thinking, but hey, he was downright thrilled. He kissed her again and again until she practically hopped on him.

"Let's go upstairs," she said. "Right now." Looked like once the lady made up her mind, she saw no reason to waste time.

He was all set to follow her upstairs to her apartment when he realized he'd forgotten something. He nodded toward Brutus. "What do I do with the furball? I can't tell him to leave us alone for a few hours."

Erin turned to look at the puppy. "Good point. Oh, I know. He stayed with me for a couple of weeks before you adopted him—"

"Technically, I didn't adopt him. The furball was forced on me."

With a smile, Erin leaned up and kissed him lightly. "You're so sexy when you pout."

"Hey, I'm not pouting. Just pointing out a fact."

She tipped her head. "Do you want to debate how you came to own Brutus, or do you want to go upstairs to my apartment?"

"I definitely want to go upstairs," he told her. "I only hope you're right about him remembering being here before. The furball likes company and is apt to drive us crazy all night if he's unhappy." The dimpled smile she gave him made it clear he'd divulged too much.

"Trent Barrett, do you let this puppy sleep with you?"

"Of course not. He sleeps…"

"In your room," she said, finishing the sentence for him.

"No. He doesn't."

"Right outside your room, then," she teased.

Actually, that was what he and Brutus had finally settled on. The furball had first jumped up on Trent's bed and made himself comfy. He'd vetoed that idea, setting the pup up on a doggy bed in the family room instead. But as soon as he'd walked away, Brutus had calmly picked up his mattress and carried it into the master bedroom.

No matter how many times he'd moved the puppy out, Brutus had come trotting back. Finally, they'd settled on Brutus sleeping by the door to his room.

"To quote you, do you really want to spend any more time talking about Brutus?" Trent asked, trailing one hand from her waist to her shoulder.

Erin gave him a quick kiss, then scooped up Brutus and headed toward the stairway. "Good point. But just so you know, I think it's adorable how much you care for this little guy. You can grumble and growl all you want, but I know you love Brutus."

Adorable? Dang. What guy wanted the woman he could hardly wait to sleep with to find him adorable? Irresistible, sure. Sexy-as-sin, absolutely. But not adorable. He was going to have to do his best over the next few hours to get Erin to rethink her image of him.

But first, they needed to deal with the furball. Erin had a doggy bed set up in the spare bedroom, and because it hadn't been that long since he'd slept in it, Brutus thankfully settled right down.

The second Erin closed the door, Trent wrapped his arms around her waist, lifted her off the ground until she was eye level with him, then said, "I'll show you who's adorable."

The kiss he gave her was deep and hot and sexy. He carried her like that with her feet off the ground down the hall and into the room he suspected was her bedroom.

Breaking the kiss, he gave her a self-satisfied male smile. "I bet you don't think I'm so adorable now."

Obviously breathless and aroused from the kiss, Erin stared at him for a couple of seconds. Then a smile slowly grew on her face.

"I wouldn't, except you just walked us into the linen closet. Now that's adorable."

Trent glanced around. Ah, man, he had. He'd taken them straight into a walk-in linen closet. So much for his lady-killer instincts.

He did the only thing a guy could do in these circumstances, he laughed.

"Dang. I give up. I'm trying to get you all excited

and turned on, and all I'm managing to do is make you think I'm adorable."

Taking his hand, she said, "This time, follow me."

"Yes, ma'am." He let her lead him out of the linen closet and down the hallway to the last room on the left.

"I should warn you, I haven't redecorated this room since I moved in. It's a little...odd."

"Does it have a bed?"

"Yes. But it's—"

"As long as it has a bed, it's great."

As soon as they entered the room, he leaned down to kiss Erin, but a flash of orange out of the corner of his eye made him stop and look around. "What the—"

The bedroom looked like a disco. The walls were painted vibrant orange and pink, with small, geometric-shaped mirrors placed all around. With a grin, Trent looked up and laughed when he saw that instead of a traditional overhead light, the room had its very own disco ball to flash splatters of light around the room.

"Now this is what I call a bedroom." He slowly studied the room. "Definitely makes you want to strut your stuff. Are you sure you didn't decorate this?"

"Hardly," she said dryly. "It looked exactly this way when I moved in. So far, all I've redone is the kitchen. I keep meaning to redo this room, but since I'm the only one who sees it—"

He grinned. "Until now."

She grinned back. "Until now. Anyway, I haven't a clue who did this. I was told when I rented the building that it had been vacant for a long time."

"Not that long." He studied the room again. "The

previous tenant was Tina Zeffner. She ran an arts and crafts shop downstairs." He walked over and turned on the disco ball. "Tina was almost eighty. She closed her shop a couple of years ago to go live by her daughter in Des Moines. The lady was always a lot of fun." He watched the globe spin overhead. "I guess I didn't realize just how much fun she was. Way to go, Tina."

"Well, if you find the room too distracting, we can go to your house," Erin offered. "Of course, we will be wasting time, but it's your call."

And Trent wasn't in the mood to waste any more time. Seeing Erin standing in the middle of this wild room with the sparkling effect of the lights dancing off the mirrors was making him crazy.

"I'm through wasting time," he said with a smile.

She smiled back. "Good boy."

❧

ERIN WOKE WITH A START. SOMETHING WAS different. She glanced down at the masculine arm wrapped around her waist.

Oh, yeah, something was most definitely different.

Hoping Trent was a sound sleeper, she tried to slowly slip free of his arm. Gingerly, she lifted a couple of his fingers in an attempt to loosen his grip. But the man proved as stubborn when asleep as he was when awake.

"Stop fussing with my hand. I like it exactly where it is," he murmured in her ear.

Unfortunately, before she could say anything, reality

returned when Brutus started yapping from down the hall.

Trent chuckled as he slowly kissed Erin. "I think the furball is getting the hang of this male bonding thing. This time, he waited until I was awake to start barking."

He gave Erin another kiss but kept it short this time. "Let me take him out for a bathroom break, then I'll be right back." He winked and added, "Don't go anywhere."

Erin laughed and assured him, "I'll wait right here."

"Thanks." As she watched Trent pull on his jeans and then head out the door to get Brutus, she leaned back in the bed, contentment filling her. She'd never been with a man just for fun before, but she had to admit, there were distinct advantages.

For starters, there were no awkward moments this morning. She and Trent had fooled around simply for pure enjoyment. And she'd had a terrific time. A really terrific time.

And now today, there were no awkward attempts at small talk. They weren't worried if the other person liked them or would fall in love with them. Instead, they were two people enjoying each other's company for as long as it lasted. Simple as that.

Trent came back into the bedroom with Brutus hot on his heels. The puppy jumped up on the bed, but Trent scooped him up and set him on the floor.

"No, stay there, furball."

Brutus wagged his tail, and after Trent sat down on the mattress next to Erin, the puppy immediately hopped up on the bed again.

"Dang, this dog is never going to learn." Trent put him on the floor again.

"Born to be wild?" Erin teased.

"Something like that." Trent leaned over and kissed Erin, but before the kiss could catch fire, Brutus jumped on the bed yet again.

"That's it," Trent said, standing and picking up the pup. "If monkeys can learn to read, you're going to learn to listen to me."

Erin couldn't help smiling because the whole time Trent was delivering his stern speech, he was scratching Brutus under the chin. The he-man chief of police was a real softy at heart.

And one heck of a nice guy.

"Brutus likes you and wants your attention," Erin said.

"Well, I like you and want your attention," Trent countered.

"I'm pretty sure if we give each other any more of our attention, neither of us will be able to walk straight."

Trent shrugged. "Walking straight is overrated in my opinion."

She laughed and tucked the sheet firmly beneath her arms when he made a move to join her once again on the bed. "Be that as it may, I have a business to run. I need to get up and dress. You and your puppy need to leave."

Trent sighed and grabbed his shirt off the floor where she'd tossed it last night. "Guess you're right, although I hate to admit it. But I need to run Brutus home and head into work myself."

After he'd gotten dressed, he kissed her one last time. "Can I see you tonight? Maybe even take you to dinner this time?"

Erin nodded. "Absolutely."

"And we're still going to the wedding together next week, right?"

The wedding. She'd completely forgotten she'd been invited to Trent's brother's wedding. When she'd agreed to go, she hadn't expected to go with him. What she had with Trent was so new, it felt odd to think about letting everyone know.

By the same token, she didn't want to keep what was happening with Trent a secret forever. She had nothing to be ashamed of, so there was no reason the world couldn't know they were seeing each other. No reason to keep it hidden.

Besides, this was Honey. Secrets lasted about as long as an ice cube in the Sahara. Sooner or later, everyone would know.

"Sure," she said.

"Great. See you tonight." With that, Trent headed out the door. She heard him talking to Brutus on the way down the stairs.

The man really was adorable.

And she could hardly wait until tonight to see him again.

❧ 8 ❧

"Your brother is here," Trent's administrative assistant, Ann Seaver, announced. "Shall I send him in?"

Trent rubbed his neck. Man, he was exhausted, but for a spectacular reason. Like every other night this week, he and Erin had spent hours making love, only to fall asleep for a little while, then wake up and make love again. The past few days with Erin had been unbelievable.

He was one happy camper today, and he didn't feel like putting up with either of his brothers or their nonsense. They'd take one look at his goofy I-had-a-great-time-last-night face and razz him like crazy.

"Tell whichever one it is that I'm not here," Trent said.

After a pause, Ann asked, "What do I do if there's two of them?"

"Both of them are here now?" He needed this like a kick to the head this morning.

"Yep. The second one just walked in. Want me to tell them you aren't here? I don't think they'll believe me since they can tell I'm talking to you, but I'm willing to give it a try."

Trent sighed, resigned to his fate. "Very cute. Fine. Send them in."

The door to his office flew open before he'd even finished speaking.

"Hey, there, baby brother," Chase said, crossing the room and dropping into one of the chairs facing Trent's desk. "You look like hell this morning."

"Good to see you, too," he said dryly, then looked at Nathan. "Go ahead. Say it. Say I look like hell."

Nathan sat in the other chair facing his desk. "You don't look like hell." He studied Trent for a second, then added with a laugh, "You look...stupidly happy. Doesn't he, Chase?"

Chase leaned back in his chair. "Why, I do believe you're right, Nathan. He does look stupidly happy. I wonder if the fact that he had lunch with Erin Weber at Roy's Café yesterday has anything to do with his expression. Megan heard from Emma that Trent and Erin looked cozier than a newlywed couple."

Ah, hell. He should have known better than to meet Erin for lunch so soon after they'd become lovers. Now the whole blasted town knew they were involved.

"Is that a fact?" Nathan smiled at Trent. "You and Erin had lunch together?"

Trent ignored the question since they obviously already knew the answer. "Why are you two bozos here? To see if I'll tell you anything?"

Chase glanced at Nathan, then back at Trent. "I

don't believe we need any answers. I think most of Honey has heard what's going on between you and Erin Weber. So much for your claim that you were never going to fall in love and get married."

Trent held up his left hand. "Do you see a ring here?"

Nathan held up his left hand. "I don't have my wedding ring on yet, either. The ceremony's not for three more days. But that doesn't mean I'm not in love and in a committed relationship."

Trent started to tell his brother that he wasn't in love, and he wasn't in a committed relationship, but for some insane reason, the words refused to pass his lips. The truth was, he might not be in love yet, but he sure did feel like he and Erin had a lot going for them.

He stared at his brothers, uncertain for the first time in his life what to say.

"We seem to have left him speechless," Chase observed. He stood and said to Nathan, "Let's leave him alone to think things over. We'll see him at the wedding on Saturday."

"Bring Erin," Nathan said.

"I'm not in love," Trent finally managed. "We're just having fun."

"Megan and I were just having fun, and now we're happily married and still having fun," Chase pointed out.

"Emma and I were just having fun, and our wedding is on Saturday," Nathan stated.

"It's different with Erin and me," Trent said, but for the life of him, that's all he could think to say.

"You just never know," Chase said. Then he headed

for the door. "Come on, Nathan. I think our work here is done. I want to head on over to the library and see if I can corner Megan in her office and make her blush."

Trent watched his brothers walk out. Despite what they thought, things really were different between him and Erin.

Weren't they?

❦

"Heck of a wedding, wasn't it?" Leigh nudged Erin. "Doesn't it make you long to walk down the aisle? To have flower girls drop rose petals at your feet? To have a handsome, wonderful man waiting to spend the rest of his life with you?"

"Not particularly," Erin said, taking a sip of her champagne. And boy did she mean it. Today's wedding had been lovely, but it had brought back more than a few memories of her own wedding day fiasco. At least Nathan Barrett had actually married Emma Montgomery, not told her he'd changed his mind and then sprinted toward the exit with the maid of honor in tow.

"No weepy moments of envy? No mental images of china patterns flashing through your mind?" Leigh prodded.

"Not a one," Erin assured her. In fact, the only images that had drifted through her mind were of the amazing things Trent had done with and to her last night. The man was phenomenally talented.

"Not even a teensy, weensy thought about wedded bliss?" Leigh continued.

Erin sighed. "Leigh, I'm not marrying your brother,

so stop pushing on me. Today's wedding was wonderful for Nathan and Emma. But I don't want to get married." Deciding to turn the tables, she asked, "What about you? Any deep-seated marital desires bubble up inside you during the ceremony?"

Leigh rolled her eyes. "Puh-lease. I'd rather remove my own appendix than tie the knot."

Okay, so maybe Erin didn't feel quite as strongly about avoiding commitment as Leigh did. But she did like her life the way it was. No strings. No ties. No heartache. Just really great sex.

It definitely worked for her.

Thinking about Trent made her wonder where he was. She glanced around the crowded wedding reception. As far as she could tell, the entire population of Honey had turned out for the wedding.

And Leigh was right—it had been a lovely ceremony. Very sweet, with the bride and groom writing their own vows and looking so very deeply in love.

Love suited some people. That was true. But it was also true that she didn't happen to be one of those people.

Erin was still searching the crowd for Trent when a pair of strong arms circled her waist from behind.

"Want to dance with the best-looking guy in the room?" Trent asked over her shoulder.

Erin leaned back against him and pretended to glance around. "Sure. Where is he?"

Leigh laughed and pointed at her brother. "You should see your expression—it's hysterical. You two are cute together. Despite what you said, Erin, I bet it won't be long before I'm at your wedding, too."

Trent's arms around her waist tightened the tiniest bit, but Erin hadn't a clue what that meant. Hopefully it meant he had as little interest in orange blossoms and wedding bands as she did. But something in his attitude the last couple of days made her wonder. He'd been acting...oddly. More interested in cuddling after love-making. More interested in talking about hopes and dreams and plans over dinner.

Not exactly the behavior of a man who was only interested in sex. Of course, she could be wrong about what he was thinking.

But when he said to his sister, "You never know what the future will bring," Erin realized maybe she wasn't wrong after all.

What kind of denial was that? Erin tipped her head and looked at him. The scary part was that he didn't seem to be kidding. But he had to be kidding. She insisted he be kidding.

"He's joking," she told Leigh firmly. Then more to Trent than to his sister, she added, "He feels the same way I do—why mess with something that's working? And what we have together is working beautifully."

From over her shoulder, Trent said, "I still believe that no one knows what the future will bring. Things change. People change. Agreements change."

Erin sighed. Oh, no. She and Trent needed to have a long, hard talk and soon. Glancing at Leigh, she asked, "Would you excuse us for a moment? I'd like to dance with your brother."

Leigh laughed. "Okeydokey. You two go dance. And let me know how your dance turns out. Keep in mind that my schedule for the fall is pretty much booked. At the moment, I only have a couple of weekends free in November and one in early December. See if any of those dates work for you." Then before Erin could once again explain that she had no interest in getting married, Leigh spotted an opening in the buffet line and bounded off.

Trent snagged Erin's hand. "Come on. I think you had a great idea. Let's dance."

Erin trailed after him, teasing as she went, "I guess I'll dance with you since that good-looking guy is nowhere to be found."

Trent flashed her a wicked grin. "Oh, you're going to pay for that later."

"I sure hope so," she said, hoping his lighthearted comment meant he'd only been kidding earlier with Leigh. He had to be kidding. Trent Barrett wasn't the type to marry and settle down. She was absolutely positive about that.

Well, close to positive.

When he took her in his arms, he slowly swayed to the music.

"Um, Trent, you know they're playing a fast song, don't you? Why are you slow dancing?"

He ran one hand up from her hip to her shoulder. "Because this way, I get to slide my hands all over you and pretend I'm just dancing instead of taking advantage of you," he said, demonstrating once again as his hand made the return journey to her hip, lingering in a few places on the way.

Erin laughed. "You're a rascal, that's for sure."

"I am, but only with you."

"For the moment," Erin said, figuring now was a

good time to clarify her feelings. "That's what's so nice about our casual relationship. There aren't any long-term expectations."

For a couple of seconds, Trent was quiet. Then he said, "We could always think about making things between us a little less casual. Like I told Leigh, things change."

Erin stopped dancing and leaned back in his arms so she could look him dead in the eyes. "Trent, don't let this wedding make you get all gushy and sentimental. We agreed we'd keep things between us simple. No strings. No ties. No broken hearts."

"First off, I'm never gushy. I'm the chief of police. I don't gush."

She hoped his nonsense meant he really wasn't getting serious on her. "Fine, you're not gushy. But there's no reason to change things between us. We're doing great. Having fun. It's perfect."

Trent started dancing again. "I can't believe I'm going to say this, but I'd kind of like things to move forward. If not completely forward, then a couple of steps in that direction."

Stunned, Erin stared at him. "Excuse me, but huh?"

"I'm talking about feelings," he said.

"You mean the kind of feeling your left hand is doing at this very moment," she couldn't resist saying, all the while hoping he'd say yes.

"No," he said. "Not that kind at all."

Drat. What were you supposed to do when a flirt like Trent Barrett got serious on you? She'd really thought he'd be the last man on earth to pull this sort of thing.

He dipped his head and whispered, "I'll admit, I have a lot of fun feeling you. Just like you seem to be enjoying yourself."

Despite the seriousness of their discussion, Erin couldn't help laughing. "But Trent, that's the only kind of feeling I'm comfortable with us doing right now."

She expected him to argue with her, but he didn't. All he said was, "Just keep an open mind, okay?"

"Fine. But for the record, my mind may be open, but I absolutely never change my mind once it's made up."

"Never?"

Her nod was firm. "Never."

"Ever?"

"Never ever," she said slowly. It was incredibly important that Trent not think she was going to want anything serious to develop between them. It simply wasn't going to happen, and the sooner he accepted that, the better. "I'm serious. I won't change my mind about this. The only reason I ever agreed to getting involved was because you don't get serious."

"I never have before," he admitted. "But like I said, things change. People change their minds."

"I won't."

"Okay. If you say so."

Despite what he'd said, Erin knew he no more believed her than he thought horses could fly.

Well, she'd simply have to show him she was serious. What they had together was fine the way it was.

No sense messing it up by getting serious.

"I CAN'T BELIEVE THIS IS HAPPENING AGAIN," ERIN SAID as she walked into Trent's office. "Here." She handed him an old straw hat with plastic grapes decorating the brim.

"And this would be?"

"You tell me. Is it another gift? I found it sitting on the hood of my car this morning."

He studied the hat. Man, it was beat-up. "And you think it was put there deliberately?"

"I think the chances of the wind blowing it and making it land on my hood are slim."

He set the hat on his desk. "I wish I'd been able to see it."

"Yeah, I know. I should have left it there and called you, but I was upset when I saw it, and I didn't think." She came over to his side of the desk and looked at the hat. "Trent, I thought this nonsense had stopped."

So had he. Nothing had happened for almost a month. He'd figured it was over with. He studied the hat. It was really ugly and looked familiar, but he couldn't place where he'd seen it before. If he had to guess, though, history said it belonged to Delia.

"So this hat was on your car. As usual, there was no note, right?"

Erin sighed. "No. No note. This is driving me crazy. Whoever is leaving these things for me is acting like a jerk. Plus, everyone in this town has known for the last month that you and I are—" She waved one hand in the air. "You know."

Trent frowned at her. He didn't like what was happening between them dismissed like that, but now wasn't the time to get into that discussion again. They'd let it drop at the wedding reception, and he didn't want to open up that can of worms right now.

Instead, he wanted to know who was leaving these things for Erin.

"Who would do this knowing I'm involved?" Erin shook her head. "It all seems too juvenile for words."

That's when it hit Trent. Juvenile. Erin was right. It did seem juvenile. Like something a person with a crush would do.

Like something a kid would do.

He grinned. "You're brilliant."

Erin gave him a dubious look. "Why? Because I'm tired of having stuff left for me by a stranger?"

"Because you've given me an idea." He kissed her soundly. "I'll stop by your store later to talk. Right now, I've got to go see someone."

"Someone who might know something about these presents?"

He nodded. "Could be."

"Who?"

Trent was tempted to tell her his idea, but he couldn't. Not until he knew if he was right. But his gut told him he was, and his gut was never wrong.

"I'll tell you later. Just head on back to your store."

Erin didn't look a bit happy about doing as he said, but she headed toward the door anyway. "I hate it when you become secretive."

"I thought women loved men of mystery," he said with a chuckle.

"Not this woman," she said right before she walked out the door.

Trent sighed. Yeah. He knew. Erin didn't love a man of mystery. She didn't love any man.

What completely amazed him was how much that bothered him. He'd never wanted a woman to care about him before, to expect things from him. He'd always figured he'd go through life without falling for anyone.

But he'd been wrong. Because he no longer could pretend he hadn't fallen for Erin. He'd fallen all right and fallen hard. Man, what a surprise.

He sighed and grabbed the hat off his desk.

Sooner or later, he was going to have to talk with Erin about how he felt. Of course, she hadn't exactly been thrilled when he'd tried to bring up the subject at the wedding reception. And he couldn't imagine she'd be happy to hear him say he'd fallen for her.

But he couldn't worry about that now. Right now, he had to go talk to someone about a hat.

ERIN BUMPED INTO LEIGH THE SECOND SHE STEPPED out of the police station.

"Hey," the younger woman said.

There was something about Leigh's expression that convinced Erin this meeting wasn't an accident. Leigh must have seen her enter the building and had planted herself outside.

"Hey to you, too." Erin turned and headed toward her shop. Not surprisingly, Leigh fell into step next to her.

After they'd taken only a couple of steps, Leigh said,

"So enough small talk. How are things between you and Trent? Am I going to be in a wedding party again soon? 'Cause if I am, you should know that I come with a lot of experience. I've married off two of my brothers this year already."

Erin kept walking. "I told you, I'm not interested in getting married. Not to anyone."

Leigh bobbed her head. "Gotcha. Not interested in marrying anyone. But Trent isn't just anyone. So are you interested in marrying him?"

"Arrrgh." Erin stopped and looked at Leigh. "What does it take to make you leave me alone about this?"

Leigh shrugged. "Marrying my brother."

"You're impossible," Erin said flatly. Then she started walking again.

"Yeah, I know I'm impossible. But that's my style. Besides, I'm curious if things will work out between you two. I've never seen Trent act like this before."

Despite herself, Erin had to ask, "Act like what?"

"Like he's crazy about a woman. He's always been footloose, but suddenly, you're all he talks about. Erin this and Erin that. It would be annoying if I didn't really like you." She grabbed Erin's arm and added, "Plus you two have been dating for almost two months. That's forever in Trent romance years. I can't remember him ever dating anyone that long. It's like..." She shrugged. "Amazing."

Trent had never dated anyone for two months? Rather than being comforted by the thought, it unnerved her.

"I don't think it's amazing," she told Leigh. "I think

it's sad that Trent's such a player he's never spent even two months with the same woman."

Leigh put her hands on her hips and snorted.

"Give me a break. He's not a player." At Erin's dubious look, she added, "Not in the sense you mean. Sure, he's always been a guy interested in fun, but do you know why?"

"He likes variety?" Erin offered, ignoring the little pang she felt when she said the words.

"No. Because when we were young, life was not a lot of fun. Dad left Mom for a waitress in town, then Mom got sick so Chase, Nathan, and Trent had to pretty much raise me. Trent got to the point where he figured life was short and damn hard. Might as well have a little fun along the way."

When all Erin did was shrug, Leigh tapped one foot on the ground. "You're looking at Trent all wrong. Okay, so he had some fun in his life. But now that he's found you, he's becoming more settled. That means something, Erin, even if you refuse to admit it."

But Erin wasn't sure she wanted it to mean anything. Sure, the more time she spent with Trent, the more she cared about him. And knowing about his background sure explained a lot about his attitude. She couldn't blame him for wanting to have a little fun when it sounded like his early years had been tough.

But she was convinced the reason she and Trent got along so well was that they kept things casual. Up until now, they'd had a great time. Not only in bed, although their sex life was wild and wonderful. No, they'd also had fun going to the movies, having dinner together, and taking Brutus for walks.

She had to admit, no matter what she and Trent were doing, they seemed to have fun. They spent a lot of time talking and laughing and truly enjoying each other's company.

Things were going well. Or they had been up until the wedding reception, when not only Leigh, but also Trent, had suggested they make their relationship something more.

Erin wasn't sure she was ready for something more. She wasn't sure she'd ever be ready.

The most frustrating part was she simply didn't know what to do. She cared for Trent, but she also was realistic about him. He was an outrageous flirt, and she couldn't see him ever settling down. Maybe in time she'd change her mind about him, but she needed that time to figure out her feelings.

There was, however, one thing that Erin was absolutely positive about. Having Leigh meddling was not good, and it needed to stop right now.

"Leigh, whatever happens is between Trent and me. I appreciate that you love your brother and want the best for him, but you need to give us breathing room."

Leigh rolled her eyes. "Breathing room. For what?"

"To..." Erin groaned. "To breathe. To make up my own mind. To make my own decisions."

"Erin, this is Honey. No one here has breathing room. That's what we all like about the town. We fit very nicely into each other's hip pocket."

"Well, I'd like everyone to get out of my pocket, thank you very much."

"You can say that all you want, but it won't happen. People in Honey like each other. We're curious about what's happening in each other's lives. We want the best for our friends and neighbors. Hence the constant curiosity. You'll get used to it."

Erin sincerely doubted that. "I appreciate your interest, Leigh, but I honestly don't know what's going to happen with Trent." And she didn't. These days, she wasn't even certain what she wanted to happen with him.

Wow, she was one confused woman.

"I need to get back to my shop," she said, wanting time alone to think.

"Fine. But remember what I said. Trent's never, ever acted this way about a woman in his whole life. It means something, Erin. Whether you want it to or not."

9

Trent found Zach sitting on the front porch of his grandmother's house all alone. Poor kid. He probably hadn't made any friends this summer since moving to town. So instead, he'd developed a crush on Erin. Not that Trent could blame the boy. Erin was one special lady.

"Hey, Zach," Trent said, coming up the walkway to stand next to the porch. In his left hand, he held the straw hat that he'd bet anything was Delia's. Zach's attention fixed on the hat, and he turned bright red. Yep, no doubt about it now. The boy was the culprit.

"Is your grandmother home?" Trent asked when Zach didn't say anything.

Zach slowly shook his head, his eyes wide, fear on his face. Trent knew if he didn't say something soon, the boy was either going to run away or cry or both.

He dropped down on the porch step next to Zach. "You know what I like about summer?"

Zach made a sniffling noise. Oh, no. Here come the tears. Trent decided to bypass them.

"I like the fact that in the summer, you can just laze around doing nothing. I think I may take today off. For instance, I'm supposed to be out finding the person who left this hat on Erin Weber's car. But maybe I'll just be lazy instead. I'm sure the person who's doing this knows it isn't right."

"Are you going to arrest..." Zach swallowed hard. "...somebody?"

"No. I'm pretty sure somebody knows to cut it out." He nudged Zach with his arm. "Don't you think so?"

Zach nodded. "Erin's nice."

"Yes, she is. But finding stuff left outside her store bothers her."

For a second, Zach once again looked like he might cry, but then he said, "I'm sorry. I thought she'd like it."

Trent dropped his arm around the boy's shoulders and gave him a quick hug. "I know."

"What are you going to do to me?"

Trent sighed. "For starters, you need to tell your grandmother what you did. Then you should tell Erin you're sorry."

Zach bobbed his head. "Okay. Do I have to go to jail, too? My grandmother won't like that."

Trent imagined not. Glancing around the yard, he noticed Zach had a soccer ball. An idea came to him. "Hey, you know what? I coach one of the boys' soccer teams. Sign-ups for the fall are going on now. If you own up to what you did by telling your grandmother and paying a visit to Erin, then I'll ask your grandmother if you can join my team. Of course, you'll have to help me with the equipment."

For the first time since Trent had arrived, Zach smiled. "I'm good at soccer. I used to play on a team in Dallas. I didn't think Honey had any teams."

"Sure we do. And we always need more players."

Noticing the time, Trent stood, and handed the hat to Zach. "Tell your grandmother she can call me if she likes."

Zach took the hat. "Okay. I really am sorry. It's just that Erin's so nice, and I really, really like her."

Trent knew exactly how the boy felt. He really, really liked Erin, too.

"Yeah, but you know, it would've never worked. Erin's thirty. Kinda old for you."

Zach looked surprised. "Oh boy. Thirty. She is old. Guess I should have realized she wouldn't fall in love with me." Then, he added, "But she's still nice. Even if she is old."

Trent laughed. Yeah, she was nice. Unfortunately, she wasn't any more likely to fall in love with him than she was with Zach.

Erin looked up as soon as Trent entered her store. He no longer had the hat with him.

"Where did you run off to? And what did you do with the hat?" She came around the counter and walked over to stand next to him.

"The hat belongs to Delia. I returned it to her grandson. Then I had a talk with the boy."

Why would he talk to Zach about the...oh. Understanding dawned on Erin. "Is he the one who's been doing all these things?"

Trent nodded. "Yep."

She never would have guessed. Zach was always so polite when he came into the store with Delia. He hardly seemed the type to leave presents on her doorstep. And now that she knew the gifts were coming from a sweet kid, Erin wasn't upset. Obviously, Zach had been trying to be nice.

"I hope you weren't mean to him. He only moved to town a few months ago when his mom came back to live with Delia. I don't think he has many friends."

Trent slipped his arms around her waist. "That's part of his punishment."

She frowned. "What?"

"He's going to join my soccer team, and he has to help me lug the team equipment to all the games. He also has to tell Delia what he did. And he has to apologize to you." He brushed a quick kiss across her lips. "That seemed like the best way to handle this. The kid didn't mean any harm, but he also needs to know he shouldn't do something like that again."

Erin stared at Trent, surprised at how thoughtful he'd been. "You're so sweet."

The grin he flashed was pure devil. "I am, aren't I? I'm a real sweetheart. Any chance I can talk you into closing your store early? I mean, after all, I did solve the crime. I ought to get a reward."

She laughed and slipped out of his arms. "I officially take back my comment. You're not sweet at all. You're incorrigible."

"No. I'm *encouragable*. One smile from you, and I am definitely encouraged." He grabbed her hand and slipped his fingers between hers. "If you can't close the store early, how about having dinner with me?"

"Um, I don't know."

"I'll cook. Heck, I'll even buy the food to cook. Now how can you possibly pass up that invitation?"

She couldn't, although she knew she should. Things with Trent were supposed to be light, casual. But they weren't turning out that way at all. They were becoming complicated. And complicated wasn't something she wanted in her life right now.

Still, how could she turn him down? He really had been terrific in the way he'd handled Zach. And she loved spending time with him. Maybe a couple more nights wouldn't hurt.

"Okay. I'll come to dinner since you're cooking and buying."

He grinned again. "Great. And I'll help you run the store until it's closing time."

"I'm not going to change my mind, so you don't have to stay and guard me," she pointed out.

Trent seemed surprised by her statement. "I'm not guarding you. I happen to want to be around you." His expression turned lecherous. "If I'm around you, then I can steal a few kisses."

He leaned down and demonstrated, and Erin didn't complain one bit. In fact, she was having so much fun kissing Trent that it took her a second to realize the bell over the front door had rung. "Oops, you've got a customer," he said.

Erin sucked a deep breath into her lungs. Yikes, but

that man could kiss. She only hoped she didn't look as wobbly as she felt. Heading toward the front of the store, she found Zach standing by the counter. Delia stood outside, peering through the glass in the front door.

"Hi," she said to Zach, who seemed to find his sneakers fascinating since he was staring at them.

"Hi," he said so quietly that Erin had to strain to hear him. Then he blurted, "I'm the one who left you all that stuff. I'm really sorry, and I'll never do it again."

Erin knew confessing was hard for Zach, but she appreciated him doing it.

"Thank you for telling me, Zach. And I know you're sorry."

She glanced over her shoulder and watched Trent walk out of the back room. Zach looked up and saw him as well. For a second, Erin was afraid seeing Trent would make Zach nervous, but instead, the boy smiled.

"I did what I promised. I told my grandma, and I apologized to Erin. So can I be on the team now?"

"You bet. I'm very proud of how you handled yourself, Zach. You showed a lot of responsibility," Trent said.

The boy beamed at the compliment, and Erin had to admit, Trent had handled this situation well. Not only had Zach learned his lesson, but he'd also learned how to take responsibility for his actions. Trent had managed all of that without making the boy feel badly about himself.

Oh, yeah, there were no two ways around it— Trent Barrett was one heck of a guy.

TRENT POPPED OPEN THE TOP TO THE PAINT CAN AND frowned. The paint was blue. A nice, ordinary, everyday blue. Dang.

"You don't want to use this paint," he told Erin. "It will make your bedroom look—"

"Normal," she said before he could finish his sentence.

"Boring, not normal. I like the room the way it is. Why are you so gung ho on changing it?" He winked at her and walked over to slip his arms around her waist. "Seems to me we've had a lot of fun in this room. I like the mirrors and the disco ball and the bright-orange paint. They put me in the mood."

To prove his point, he kissed her. But before he could woo her into a little hanky-panky, she gently removed his hands from her oh-so-soft body.

"As far as I can tell, anything puts you in the mood," she said with a laugh. "Last week, you pounced on me when we were discussing the best way to cook shrimp."

"Hey, cooking makes me hot."

She laughed. "You're insane."

"Probably, but knowing my family, does that come as a surprise?"

Ha. He had her there, and he knew it.

"No," she admitted. "Not at all. Now stop pouting and help me paint the room." With a sexy little smile that got his blood pounding through his veins, she said, "The sooner we're done, the sooner I'll reward you for all your manly effort."

"Incentive. I like that. What did you have in mind?"

She pretended to think. Finally, she said, "I know; I'll make dinner for you."

"Dinner? Not exactly what I had in mind. Try again. I'm going to need a serious bribe to get me to agree to paint these pretty orange walls a dull blue."

With great exaggeration, she fluttered her eyelashes at him. "Why, Mr. Barrett, what could I possibly have that would be of interest to you?"

He chuckled. "I'm going to enjoy showing you later."

"Fine. But first you have to help." She poured paint into both of their trays. "You want to do the baseboards or start on the walls?"

"I'll do the walls. If I'm not allowed to touch you until this room is done, then I want to get it finished in a hurry," he said, meaning it. Although he liked just spending time with Erin, he also was burning with need for her. He'd been stuck at work late last night and hadn't been able to see her. After only two days, he'd missed her so much it hurt.

He started rolling the paint onto the walls, figuring if he had to keep his hands to himself for the next hour or so, then he could at least use the time to talk to her about how he felt. Now all he had to think of was a subtle way to start a conversation about their relationship. Subtle wasn't exactly his strong point, but there had to be a way to do it After forty-five frustrating minutes during which no brainstorms rained on him, he blurted, "So, Erin, what's new with you?"

She was carefully painting the baseboard by the closet with a nice white paint. Now she turned her head and looked at him. "What?"

Yeah, he deserved the strange look she was giving him. Dang, he was handling this all wrong.

He admitted the truth. "I'm trying to find a nonchalant way to bring up our relationship."

"Ah."

That was it. That was all she said. Then she turned back to painting the baseboard.

Trent went back to painting the walls. But frustration churned inside him until, with a groan, he turned to face her. "So do you?"

"Do I what?"

"Want to discuss what's happening between us." Granted, he'd never before had a relationship like the one he had with Erin, but he'd always heard women liked to talk about their relationships. But, man, if the expression on Erin's face was anything to go by, she'd rather be dunked in mud and hosed down with grease than talk about the two of them.

"Why can't we just leave everything the way it is? Why does it have to change?" she asked softly.

"Because I've changed," he admitted.

She tipped her head and studied him. "How?"

For a second, he almost decided not to tell her. After all, he knew she didn't want to hear what he had to say. But he'd never backed down from anything in his entire life, and he sure wasn't going to start now.

"I'm in love with you," he said.

She blinked. A couple of times. Then she asked slowly, "You're in love with me? Are you sure?"

Was he sure? Hell, yes, he was sure. "Well, I'm in love with someone, and it sure isn't Brutus." This wasn't going at all the way he'd wanted it to go. He hadn't expected her to say she loved him in return, but then again, he hadn't expected her to look horrified by the idea, either.

"Erin, why are you so surprised? We've been dating for the last couple of months. We spend all our free time together. We spend almost every night together. Is it really so unbelievable that I'd fall in love with you?"

She nodded her head. "Yes. It is. I mean that was the whole point of us. We knew we wouldn't fall in love. We agreed we'd keep it simple. No strings. Your being in love with me is a really big string, Trent."

"Tell me about it. I didn't do this on purpose. I've never even thought I was in love before let alone actually been in it. It's...weird. I know I should feel panicky and nervous, but I'm not. Actually, the opposite. I feel good. Incredibly good. Like I've found a missing piece of a puzzle."

Erin's expression softened a little at his description, but she still didn't seem too thrilled by the whole love thing.

Figuring he was in for some serious pain, Trent asked, "Don't you feel anything for me?"

She set the brush carefully on the side of the paint tray and said, "Of course I do."

Okay. That wasn't much, but at least it was something. "What do you feel?"

"I like and admire you, and I think you're a great guy," she said with a soft smile.

Although he appreciated the sentiment, those sure weren't the words he'd wanted to hear.

"Erin, I've never told a woman I love her before. I've never even come close to love. My entire life, I've avoided it like a big old tar pit. But this much I know—we're great together. And we're great for each other. I can't help thinking we're meant to be together. You honestly don't feel the connection between us? There's a lot more going on between us than just killer sex, and you've got to know that."

A light blush colored her cheeks. "Of course, I know we're great together. But I also thought Don and I were great together. That we were meant to be together. That is, until he sprinted from the church."

"Hey, I'm not Don."

"I know that. But I'm still me," she said.

She'd lost him there. "What does that mean?"

"It means, I need more time. Sure, things between us seem to be going great. But things between Don and me seemed great, too. I completely misjudged our relationship. Heck, I completely misjudged him, too. Do you know he's divorcing the woman he left me for? I used to be so certain that Don was a steady, dependable guy. Shows you how bad of a character judge I am."

"Thanks for the compliment," Trent said dryly.

"You know what I mean."

"I don't think I do." He wasn't the type to get upset about things usually. In fact, that was one of the main reasons he found being chief of police enjoyable. He rarely got upset. But he sure was upset now.

"Trent, I just need time," she said, coming over to stand next to him. "Is that so much to ask?"

"It is because you want this time so you can figure out that I'm not the same kind of jerk as your ex-fiancé. Well, you should know that by now. I shouldn't have to prove it to you."

135

"I don't mean it like that," she said.

But he knew she did. She needed time because she wasn't sure. But he couldn't help thinking she should be sure by now.

"Let's forget about it and finish painting this room," he said.

She didn't say anything, so he turned his attention back to the walls, quickly finishing the painting. Then he set the roller down and headed toward the door.

"You know where to find me if you ever decide I'm not a jerk," he said.

"Trent, wait."

He stopped, turning slightly to look at her.

"I just need more time," she said. "Maybe then I'll change my mind and want a relationship."

He sighed, feeling incredibly defeated. "You know, Erin, I never believed in love before I met you. Never believed there was one perfect person for everyone. But I've changed my mind. I now think that when something's meant to be, it's meant to be. And when you find something this great, you need to be brave enough to grab hold of it and not let go."

He willed himself not to weaken when a couple of tears slipped free and rolled down her face.

"I'm not letting go," she said. "You are."

"That's just because you're not willing to hold on," he told her.

Then he left.

"Mind if I join you?"

Erin glanced up from the menu she'd been studying. Megan Barrett, Chase Barrett's wife, stood next to the table. The last thing Erin wanted to do at the moment was talk about Trent. She'd spent the better part of a week thinking about him. And even after all that thinking, she still wasn't certain how she felt.

But good manners forced her to say to Megan, "Not at all. Please sit."

Megan took the chair across from Erin and opened her own menu. "I never know why I look at the menu each time I come to Roy's Cafe. I mean, it's not like I haven't eaten here a million times before. And since nothing on the menu ever changes, it's not like I don't already know what my choices are." She smiled over the menu at Erin. "Guess I keep hoping something better than my current choice will appear."

Erin frowned. Was that a veiled message of some sort or just a vocalized wish for more variety on the menu? She started to ask Megan, but the one waitress in the cafe stopped by and took their order. Megan ordered what she'd obviously ordered the million other times when she'd been here before.

After the waitress walked away, Megan leaned back in her chair. "Are you enjoying Honey?"

That didn't seem like a loaded question, so Erin said, "Yes. It's a nice town."

"It is, isn't it? Very friendly. Filled with wonderful people."

Erin frowned again. Was Megan once more saying something without actually saying something?

It seemed difficult to believe considering that every time she'd ever talked to Megan before, the woman had been very open and friendly. Surely she wasn't trying to nudge Erin in Trent's direction. Was she?

"When I first moved here, I was eight years old," Megan said. "I didn't know a soul, and I had quite a bit of trouble with a town bully. But then one day, Chase showed up and scared off the bully for me. I fell in love with him in that split second, and I've never fallen out of love with him."

Okay, this time there was no doubt. The woman was here on a mission.

"Megan, no offense, but I don't really want to talk about Trent."

"I wasn't talking about Trent," the other woman said. "Just talking about when I first moved to Honey."

"And when you fell in love with your husband," Erin added.

"Oh, yes. But I only mentioned that because I wanted you to know what a great guy Chase is."

Erin sighed. "And naturally you think Trent is a great guy, too."

"Yes, he is," Megan said. They sat quietly while the waitress placed their lunches in front of them. As soon as they were alone again, she said, "He really is a great guy, Erin."

"I take it he told you what happened?"

Megan nodded. "Sort of. Actually, his brothers dragged the information out of him, which is pretty much the way that family works. But yes, I know he's in love with you, but you don't love him back."

Erin opened her mouth to respond, then suddenly realized the entire cafe had gone silent. Pin-drop silent.

She glanced around. Everyone was obviously listening to her conversation with Megan.

What was with this town?

As softly as possible, she said to Megan, "I told him it's possible I'll eventually come to love him. All I asked was for a little more time."

Apparently, she hadn't been quite quiet enough because a low buzz of gossip erupted when she finished speaking.

"What'd she say?" someone in a far corner asked. Erin felt like banging her head against the table when someone answered, "She said she doesn't love Trent."

She looked at Megan. "You'd think if they were going to eavesdrop, they'd get it right." Turning, she said to the crowd, "I said it's possible I may come to love him. Eventually."

The patrons of the restaurant pretended they were interested in their own meals and hadn't been listening to her, but as soon as she turned back around to face Megan, she heard the person in the corner ask, "What'd she mean by eventually?"

"Don't let them upset you," Megan said gently. "They just really like Trent and want him to be happy."

"Leigh already shared the hip-pocket philosophy of this town with me," Erin said.

"It's a mixed blessing," Megan admitted. "So you were saying that you may eventually come to love Trent before we got distracted. What exactly does that mean?"

"It means I need time."

Megan nodded, and for a second, Erin thought the

other woman might understand. At least she did until Megan asked, "Time for what?"

"To figure out my feelings for him."

"Okay. So you need time. Mind if I ask you a question?"

Truthfully, Erin minded this entire conversation, but at this juncture, she didn't see much point in protesting. "Sure. Ask away."

"What is Trent supposed to do while you're figuring out whether you love him or not?"

Erin stared at the other woman, dumbfounded. She'd never considered that before. What did she expect Trent to do while she had more time to think about their relationship? Did she expect him to wait for her? To keep seeing her on the chance that she might one day love him, too? Or did she expect him to start dating someone else, someone who could quickly decide whether she was in love or not.

She honestly had no idea.

"I don't know," she admitted. Then listened while her answer was relayed to the person in the corner who was obviously hard of hearing. What a town.

Megan patted her hand. "Why don't you figure that out. I think once you know what you expect Trent to do, then you'll also know how you feel about him."

With a nod, Erin turned back to her salad. She wasn't hungry anymore because Megan had given her a lot to think about. But for the sake of appearances, she pretended to eat her salad.

But her mind wasn't on food. It wasn't even on the fact that the entire cafe was now openly discussing what she'd said. Most of the room seemed to be of the opinion that she should marry Trent. A few ladies, though, firmly maintained that Trent wasn't the type to settle down.

But Erin couldn't listen to them chatter at the moment. Her mind was on Trent. What in the world was she going to do about him?

She really had no idea. None at all. But she knew Megan was right. Once she knew what she expected Trent to do while she made up her mind, then she'd know what her feelings were for him. Right now, she had no answers. But hopefully she would soon.

For her sake. For Trent's sake.

She sighed. And based on the heated discussions going on in the cafe, for the sake of the town as well.

❧ 10 ❧

Trent rubbed Brutus' belly, glad the puppy had finally stopped throwing up. Man, but that dog had been sick. A couple of times during the last few hours, he'd been really worried about the furball. He'd ended up taking him to the vet just to make certain Brutus was going to be all right.

Who'd have ever thought he'd come to care this much about the puppy?

He knew the answer—Erin had. All along she'd told him he'd come to love Brutus, and he did. Brutus seemed to love him right back. All it had taken was being nice to the puppy, and Brutus had come right around.

Too bad he couldn't figure out a way to make Erin love him as well.

"Maybe if I sit with her when she's sick, she'll decide she loves me," he said to the dog.

Brutus flopped his tail once, a sure sign he still wasn't one hundred percent better. Poor little guy. This was all Leigh's fault. She should have been watching him closely. Then she would have seen Brutus eat the dead crickets.

"Women," Trent said, still rubbing the puppy's stomach. "They'll let you eat crickets and break your heart all without batting an eye." Brutus sighed a big puppy sigh, obviously agreeing with Trent.

"I mean, come on. I told her I loved her. I've never told another woman that ever." Warming to his topic, Trent added, "I went out on a limb, put my feelings out there for her to see, and she said she needed time."

Brutus made a hmpf noise which Trent took as a dog's version of a snort.

"Exactly. That's what I want to know. Time for what? To see if I'm a jerk?" He scratched the puppy behind the ears. "See if I'm the same sort as her ex-fiancé? What about faith? What about trust? Don't those count for anything? Haven't I convinced her that I'm nothing like that Don guy? Haven't I shown her I really love her?"

He looked at Brutus. "You know, I'm going to go have another talk with her. I thought I'd let this sleeping dog lie, but I can't. I'm not giving up. Not yet. Not by a long shot. I'm the right guy for her, and if she doesn't see that, then I'll have to help her see that. I've never been in love before, and I know in my bones, I'll never be again."

He glanced again at Brutus and saw that the puppy had finally fallen asleep. Since the furball was asleep on the guest bedroom floor, Trent decided to sleep in here as well. He wanted to be nearby just in case the pup had more trouble during the next few hours.

And then tomorrow, once he had taken Brutus to the vet again to make certain the pup really was all right, he was going to go see Erin.

Things between them weren't over. Not nearly over. In fact, even with everything that had happened over the last couple of weeks, he couldn't help believing that things between him and Erin were just beginning, not ending.

They were meant to be together. He was absolutely positive of that.

ERIN WAS FEEDING THE HAMSTERS WHEN THE BELL over the door jangled. Leigh Barrett walked in, her expression determined. Uh-oh. That couldn't be good. Leigh at the best of times was like a human tornado. A determined Leigh could only be big trouble.

"Hi," Erin said, hoping against hope that she'd misread Leigh's expression. Maybe the younger woman wasn't here on a mission.

"Sick puppy," Leigh said. "One sick puppy."

Okay, now that seemed way too harsh. "Excuse me?"

"Do you know what Trent's been doing all night?" Leigh asked in return.

"I don't know, Leigh, but whatever it is, it won't change my mind. I've told every member of your family and most of the town of Honey that I really care about Trent, but I don't think it's a good idea for us to get too serious. We had agreed when we first started—"

"Messing around?" Leigh supplied.

"Not exactly the way I would have put it, but yes.

We both agreed we weren't interested in getting serious." Trying one more time to get the other woman to see her viewpoint, Erin explained, "It wasn't all that long ago that I thought I'd found the perfect man for me. It turned out to be a disaster. I was completely wrong about him and only saw what I wanted to see. I'm not looking for more heartache."

Leigh nodded thoughtfully, then said slowly, "Sick puppy."

Okay, that was it. "I'm not a sick puppy just because I don't want to have my heart smushed by your brother."

"Of course you're not a sick puppy. Brutus is. That's what Trent's been doing the entire night— tending to the sick puppy."

The puppy was sick? The little guy had been the picture of health and mischief the last time Erin had seen him.

"What's wrong with Brutus?"

"He ate some dead crickets and has been grossly sick all night."

"How was he able to eat the dead crickets? Trent always watches Brutus carefully."

Leigh's gaze darted around the shop. "Someone had taken him for a walk and her...I mean, that person's cell phone rang. That person was talking about a real cool job offer, and for one split second didn't watch the dog."

Erin sighed. "Leigh, you have to watch Brutus all the time. He's like a goat. He'll eat anything."

"Hey, goats do not eat just any old thing."

"But Brutus does," Erin pointed out.

Leigh drummed her fingers on the counter beside

her. "We're getting off the main point here. It doesn't matter how Brutus got sick, just that he was. And my brother drove him to the vet in the middle of the night, then sat up with him until morning."

She leaned toward Erin and added, "Plus, he even rearranged his schedule so he could stay home from work today and make certain the little guy is better."

Trent had done all that for the puppy? Heck, adopting Brutus hadn't even been his idea.

"Does he know you're here?" Erin asked.

With a snort, Leigh said, "As if. He'd bust a vein if he knew. But when I went over there this morning and saw what he'd been up to, well, I had to come and tell you. You're all wrong about Trent. Sure, he can be a little wild. Maybe a lot wild. But he's a good guy. He's nothing like that jerk you were engaged to marry."

"I appreciate what you're doing. It's very sweet of you to come defend your brother. I agree that Trent is a great guy. He's smart and funny and can be unbelievably sweet. But I'm not looking for a serious relationship right now. I've just moved to this town and opened my business. Love can wait."

"No, it can't. And it won't. Love doesn't stick around where it's not wanted. If you don't grab hold of the love Trent's offering you, it will disappear. And you'll be left alone and sorry."

With that pronouncement, Leigh spun on one heel and headed toward the door.

"Leigh—"

The younger woman stopped and turned. "Do you realize you're walking away from a man who's willing to clean up after a sick puppy? A really sick puppy filled with dead cricket parts. Come on, how many guys do you know would clean up that kind of mess, especially when they didn't really want the dog in the first place?" She shook her head. "You're never going to find anyone else even half as great as Trent is, and you know it. He's loyal to his job. He's loyal to his family. For crying out loud, he's loyal to Brutus. He'd be loyal to you, too."

Then Leigh yanked open the door and walked out.

"Guess I've been told," Erin muttered to the hamsters after the door slammed shut behind Leigh. One of the small, furry pets seemed to stare directly at her, almost as if he were listening.

"But I'm right," she said.

The hamster tipped his head and looked as doubtful as a hamster can look. Great. Even small rodents thought she was being a fool.

"Fine, maybe I am a fool, but just because someone loves you doesn't mean you have to love him back." The hamster continued to watch her with his small black eyes. "Oh, all right, even if I do love him, that doesn't mean we have to get married and have a couple of kids and buy a minivan and go to soccer games. We're not required to live happily ever after."

She said the last sentence with enough force that the hamster wiggled his nose and ran off. Apparently, he was unconvinced by her argument.

Well, too bad. It was a good argument. A sound argument. So maybe Trent wasn't like Don. Maybe he wouldn't run off with another woman. Maybe once he settled down, he really would be settled for life.

Did that mean she had to be the woman he settled down with?

Of course not.

Feeling unbelievably dejected but refusing to give in to the mood, she finished feeding the hamsters, then moved on to the fish. Thankfully, none of them looked at her with accusatory eyes. They blithely went about their fish lives, ignoring her.

"You don't care a bit that my heart's broken," she said, shaking more food into the fish tank. When what she'd just said hit her, she froze.

Her heart was broken? Really? When had that happened? Why hadn't she noticed when the first tiny fracture lines had appeared?

This was exactly what she'd been trying to avoid—a broken heart. She'd gone to great lengths to prevent this very circumstance. She'd moved to a new town. Started all over again. Gotten involved with the one man who absolutely would not break her heart.

And yet she'd still ended up hurt because what she hadn't counted on was how crazy in love she'd be with Trent. He was so wonderful; how could she not love him? The man had sat up all night with a sick puppy. Who could resist a guy that terrific?

Not her. The only reason her heart was broken was that she refused to accept the love he was freely offering.

"I really am a fool," she told all the animals in general, realizing she'd been avoiding facing the truth for a long, long time. So her ex-fiancé had been a jerk, and sure, it seemed way too soon to get involved again.

But Trent was a different man than Don. A man she knew in her heart she could trust.

She didn't need any more time to know that. She didn't need any more proof of his love.

She just needed him.

"Well, that's a problem I can fix." And she could. All she had to do was say yes. Yes to loving him. Yes to spending her life with him.

She could do that. In fact, she could hardly wait to do that.

Glancing at the clock, she saw she had three hours before it would be time to close the store. She could only hope those hours went quickly because she could hardly wait to see Trent.

TRENT HEADED DOWN THE SIDEWALK AT A CLIP. HE'D spent a long night thinking about this whole thing with Erin, and dang it all, he was going to say what was on his mind. She was making one huge mistake keeping them apart, and he was going to let her know that.

Feeling stoked, he shoved open the door to Precious Pets and headed inside. Erin was with Delia and Zach, apparently helping them pick out some more bird food, but he didn't care. For once in his life, he was going to ignore his mama's teachings and be downright rude.

"Excuse me, Delia and Zach, but can I have a few minutes alone with Erin? We need to talk." He planted his feet firmly and knew she could tell he meant business.

Rather than looking upset, Erin seemed pleased.

Well, she probably wouldn't be once he was done, but at least she'd know how he felt.

"I'm so glad you stopped by," she said. "I want to talk to you, too."

Now that was a change in her tune. But before he could get his hopes up, he reminded himself that she'd probably just thought of another reason why the two of them had no future. Well, whatever she'd come up with, he'd find a counterargument. He might not be the brightest searchlight in the sky, but he knew they should be together, and he wasn't giving up or backing down.

He glanced at Delia, who flashed him a wide grin. She obviously knew he was a man on a mission.

"I'll stop by tomorrow for the seed, Erin." She nudged her grandson, who was looking from Trent to Erin then back to Trent. "Come on, Zach. Let's go look for soccer shin guards for you."

"Great." Zach must have figured out what was going on, too, because on his way by Trent, he said, "Good luck."

Trent patted the boy's shoulder. Yeah. Good luck. He could use some of that.

Delia winked. "Remember, you have handcuffs if you need to get her to stand still and listen to you."

Then, with a laugh, Delia and her grandson headed out the door. Once they were alone, Trent faced Erin. She still looked very happy, and for a split second, he worried that the speech he'd worked up would make her unhappy. But he pushed that thought aside. She definitely needed to hear what he had to say.

"Isn't this how we met? You standing there with your handcuffs, all set to arrest me?" Erin asked, a twinkle in her eyes.

"I wasn't going to arrest you. I just had some questions."

She smiled. "And today? Do you have questions?"

Yeah, he had one. One very important question. But first, they needed to get some things straight. Trent squared his shoulders and took two deliberate steps forward until he stood toe-to-toe with Erin. "We need to talk."

She arched one brow and didn't look the least bit intimidated. "Oh, really?"

"Yes, really. I've had a long night, and I've done a lot of thinking. I've come to a few important conclusions."

"Okay. Such as?"

At least she was being reasonable about this. "For starters, just because we originally thought we'd keep things casual doesn't mean they always have to stay that way. Life is about change, Erin. And when something wonderful happens, you don't push it away because you didn't expect it. You grab on to it with both hands even if it wasn't part of your original plan."

She nodded. "I know."

She did? Well...good. But he wasn't nearly done. "And you're dead wrong about me. I'm not the kind of guy who would tell a woman he loved her if he didn't mean he'd love her forever."

Erin gave him a soft smile. "I know."

Momentarily disconcerted, he gathered his thoughts, running through the other points he'd come up with during the long night. Oh, there was another really important one.

"You also don't give yourself enough credit. It wasn't your fault that your ex-fiancé was a moron. You're a trusting person, and you thought you'd found someone who was equally trustworthy. That doesn't mean your judgment in men is off. It just means you had the bad luck to choose the wrong guy."

Her smile grew. "I know."

She did? He ran one hand through his hair. "But that guy wasn't the right guy. I'm the right guy. I've never told a woman I loved her. I've never even come close. This is the real deal, Erin, and you can't let it pass us by."

She leaned closer to him. "I know."

For crying out loud, what was going on here? Was this some sort of game? She'd made it clear time and again that she didn't agree with him, so why wasn't she putting up a fight now?

He blew out an exasperated breath. "Why are you agreeing with everything I'm saying?" "Because I think you're right."

He frowned. "Since when?"

She laughed. "You simply can't believe that I agree with you, can you?"

"No. Not really. You never have before," he pointed out.

She placed one hand on his arm. "I do now. Earlier, I reacted without thinking. But when I really stopped to consider everything, I realized you aren't my ex-fiancé. And I truly believe you're the right man for me."

Dang. Now he knew something was up. "Not that I'm not thrilled with what you're saying, 'cause I am. But I have to ask—what changed your mind?"

"Leigh did."

Ah, hell. If Leigh was involved, this couldn't be

good. He stared at Erin, hoping he'd heard her wrong. Although he loved Leigh, he couldn't exactly say she'd been a big help in his life. In fact, he could readily think of about a hundred times when she'd caused him trouble. The woman was a walking disaster zone.

"Are we talking about my sister Leigh?" he asked, just to make certain.

Erin laughed. "Don't be so cynical. Of course, I mean your sister."

"I'm not cynical. I'm just trying to figure out what Leigh could have possibly done to make you agree with me."

With one small step, Erin moved close enough to lean against him. "Leigh told me how you took care of Brutus last night."

What did the sick pup have to do with all of this? "Of course, I took care of the furball. He was sick and needed me."

"Exactly. You were there for Brutus. Just like you're always there for everyone who needs you. At first, I thought you were a hopeless flirt and a wild man. But over the past few months, I've come to realize that you're actually a great guy. Leigh told me about how you took care of Brutus through the night. It reminded me just how great you are."

He liked the sound of that. Things were definitely moving in the right direction. "So since you think I'm great, where does that leave us?"

"First, I have to ask how Brutus is."

Trent laughed. "Figures. I'm standing here more nervous than I've ever been in my life, and you're talking about the furball."

She placed one hand on the side of his face. "You love Brutus, and you know it."

"Yeah. I do," he admitted. "He's grown on me. And to answer your question, he's fine. Under the weather last night, but perky as all get-out today. I took him to the vet this morning and was assured he's out of the woods."

"Good. I'm so glad to hear that," she said.

"So now that you know Brutus has recovered, I'd like to return to the conversation about us. I believe you were saying how great you think I am."

She looked downright adorable when she gave him a flirty, sexy look. Man, he loved this woman. "I do think you're great."

"That's it?"

"No. I love you, too."

At her words, his heart raced in his chest. She loved him. Just to make certain, he asked, "Sure?"

She nodded. "Positive."

Life did not get any sweeter than this. He leaned down and kissed her. For several long minutes, he simply held her in his arms and enjoyed kissing the woman he loved. Finally, he broke the kiss but still held her firmly within the circle of his arms.

"So what happens now? You said you needed more time."

She shook her head. "Not anymore."

He took a deep breath and plunged ahead. "So if I ask you to marry me, is there any chance you'll say yes?"

"Um, are you asking me or just asking me if it's okay to ask me?"

"Whatever's the best way to get a yes," he admitted.

"Just ask," she said softly.

He readily complied. "Will you marry me?"

"Yes."

He grinned. All right! He was about to kiss her again when he felt obligated to admit, "You know Brutus is part of this deal, and I can't promise he's completely house trained yet. I've tried, but that dang furball has a mind of his own."

She laughed. "I think I can help with that problem."

"Oh. Good. Then we can tell everyone we're getting married for the sake of the dog," Trent teased.

"That and because I'm crazy about you."

Trent couldn't remember ever feeling this fantastic. "I'm crazy about you, too. And you'll see. We really will live happily ever after because you're the right woman for me, Erin. I've never felt this way before, and I know I never will again."

"I know. You're meant for me." She wrapped her arms around his neck. "And I'm meant for Trent."

He chuckled. "I like the sound of that. It's corny, sure, but effective."

"And oh, so very true," she said right before she kissed him.

☙❧

DEAR READER,

Readers are an author's life blood and the stories couldn't happen without *you*. Thank you so much for reading! If you enjoyed *Handsome Lawman* we would so appreciate a review. You have no idea how much it means to us.

If you'd like to keep up with our latest releases, you can sign up for Lori's newsletter @ https://loriwilde.com/sign-up/.

Please turn the page for an excerpt of the fourth book The Handsome Devil series, Handsome Cowboy.

To check out our other books, you can visit us on the web @ www.loriwilde.com.

EXCERPT: HANDSOME COWBOY

She was going to kill her brothers. All three of them. Slowly. In front of the entire town of Honey, Texas.

How dare they invite Jared Kendrick to Trent's wedding? No, not only invite him, but also have him in the wedding party. Were they insane? Was this some kind of lame joke?

Whatever the cause, they were dead men for sure.

"The wedding was beautiful," said Amanda Newman, wife of the minister who'd performed the ceremony. "Trent and Erin seem so happy. Now all your brothers are blissfully married. Guess it won't be long until you follow their example."

Leigh barely resisted the urge to gag. As if. She'd rather go swimming with piranha. Here she'd finally married off her last meddlesome brother, and from this point on, she'd be an independent woman.

No way was she giving up her freedom anytime in this century.

"I'm too young to get married," she told Amanda.

Standing on her tiptoes, she scanned the wedding reception crowd, looking for her brothers.

How hard was it to spot three tall men in tuxes? Apparently impossible, since she didn't see them.

Maybe the weasels were hiding from her. Yeah. That was a distinct possibility. At least it was if they had the slightest inkling as to what she was thinking at the moment.

"Oh, now I'm sure this wedding is giving you ideas." Amanda patted Leigh's arm and smiled. "I can see you're studying the decorations, maybe coming up with plans for your own reception."

Leigh stared at her, stunned. Amanda was a sweet older woman, but boy, she didn't have a clue what Leigh was thinking. Not that she could exactly enlighten her. After all, how did you tell the minister's wife that you were looking for your brothers so you could kill them? Hmmm. Emily Post probably didn't have any etiquette advice for this particular circumstance.

Deciding not to go into it, Leigh said, "I'm not interested in getting married. Thanks."

Figuring that was settled, she returned to scanning the crowd. Where were those bozos? She finally spotted two of her sisters-in-law, Megan and Emma, over by the buffet table. Wherever they were, their husbands and her brothers, Chase and Nathan, wouldn't be far behind.

Bingo. She'd found them.

She started to head in that direction when Amanda once again put her hand on Leigh's arm. "Getting married and starting your own family is one of life's precious gifts," Amanda said. "As I know your brothers have discovered."

Leigh bit back a groan. Would this woman never stop? She didn't want to get married. She didn't want to fall in love.

She only wanted to talk to her ratfink brothers and then maybe kick Jared Kendrick out of here. Was that too much to ask for?

"No offense, Amanda, 'cause I know you're happily married," Leigh said. "But I have no desire to live in a house with a white picket fence."

"Do tell. Because I could have sworn that the house you're renting from Megan has a white picket fence out front," a deep voice said from behind her.

Oh, just great. While she'd been looking for her brothers, Jared Kendrick had walked up and was apparently standing directly behind her. Man-o-man, this day just kept getting worse.

"Hello, Jared," Amanda said. "I heard you moved back to Honey. You're turning your parents ranch into a rodeo school, right?" Without waiting for an answer, Amanda continued. "Mary Monroe said she saw you riding that motorcycle of yours around town. And she said you were going quite fast. I told her you probably weren't, but I don't think she believed me."

Leigh rolled her eyes. Of course, the man had been driving fast This was Jared Kendrick. If there was a rule in Honey, he broke it

"I might have been going a couple of miles over the speed limit," Jared admitted. "Tell her I'll slow down from now on."

Unable to stop herself, Leigh snorted. "That will be the day."

"Hello to you, too," Jared said.

Turning slowly, Leigh braced herself for the wallop she knew she'd feel when she made eye contact with this man. Despite no longer liking him, she was still female. And females of all ages found it difficult to resist Jared. He was tall, over six feet, and had amazingly thick dark brown hair and equally dark eyes. The man was serious eye candy.

Dang his hide.

Predictably, as soon as Leigh looked at him, her DNA betrayed her. Her stupid heart raced. Her equally stupid breathing seemed to have grown rapid and shallow.

This world was one screwy place when the man you disliked more than any other turned you on like crazy.

Sheesh.

Taking a deep breath to calm her raging libido, she flashed him a completely insincere smile. "Why, hello, Kendrick. I thought you'd be in jail by now. Did the Parole Board take a liking to you?"

Jared laughed, the sound deep and rich and way too appealing. "Glad to see you haven't changed since last summer, Leigh."

Amanda frowned and made a tsking sound. "Oh, Jared, were you really in jail? My, my. I thought you were riding with those rodeo people. Of course, you were a trifle wild while growing up here, but I had no idea you'd run into serious trouble."

Leigh waited patiently for Jared to correct the older woman and explained he hadn't been in jail, but he simply shrugged. Oh, for the love of Pete. Was he really going to let this go? The Honey rumor mill would have a field day. Leigh knew that before the night was over, all the good folks of Honey would swear up and down that Jared had been in jail for murder.

"Maybe my husband could counsel you," Amanda offered. "He's very good with things like his."

Leigh groaned. "Amanda, Jared wasn't in jail. I was kidding."

Amanda laughed softly, and Leigh rolled her eyes.

"Oh, good. You two are joking," Amanda said. 'I'm happy to hear that. Although I will admit I was surprised to see you in the wedding party today. I didn't know you were friends with Trent."

"Everyone seemed surprised to see me," he said. Leigh more so than most. I especially liked the way she screamed when she noticed me standing next to her brothers by the altar. You'll have to check with your husband, Amanda, but I bet she's the first bridesmaid to scream like that during a ceremony."

"Oh, pulleese. I'm sure a lot of women scream around you," Leigh said, and then she felt like whacking herself on the side of the head when she realized the interpretation that could be put on her words. From the grin on Jared's face, he'd taken it as a compliment to his lovemaking prowess.

Leigh shook her head. "Hey! Don't go there. I only meant—"

Jared held up one hand and drawled, "I know exactly what you meant, Leigh, and thanks. Maybe one day you can find out for yourself if it's true."

Keenly aware that Amanda was watching them

Leigh said in her sweetest voice, "Kendrick, I'd rather two-step with a rattlesnake. No, wait, it wouldn't be much different, would it?"

Amanda frowned and looked from Leigh to Jared then back at Leigh. "What are you talking about dear? Are you teasing Jared again?"

A sexy grin slowly crossed Jared's handsome face. "Yeah, Leigh, are you teasing me again?"

"I'm completely, absolutely sincere," she said firmly, which only made Jared grin more.

Typical.

"Oh." Amanda looked confused. "I see. Well, I guess we'd better find our seats now. It looks like the toasts are about to start," Amanda pointed out.

Leigh glanced around. People were quickly finding their places at the small round tables. With quick goodbye to Amanda, Leigh headed over to the table near the front where she was supposed to sit. Now she'd have to wait until later to talk to her brothers, but at least she'd be away from Jared.

Boy, he really got to her. Big time. Why in the world had her doofus brothers invited him to be in the wedding party? Had love turned their brains to mush? They hated Jared, and ever since their dating fiasco a few months back, he was the last man she ever wanted to see again.

So what in the world was he doing here?

And why in the blazes did he still get to her so much?

EXCERPT: HANDSOME RANCHER

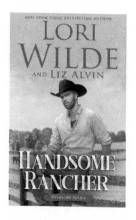

As she studied him, standing near the entrance to the city council room, Megan Kendall couldn't help thinking what a handsome devil Chase Barrett was.

Everyone in the small town of Honey, Texas, thought so as well. With his drop-dead gorgeous looks and his handsome-devil smile, women fell for him like pine trees knocked down by a powerful tornado.

Even Megan couldn't claim to be immune. She and

Chase had been good friends for over twenty years, and he still didn't know she was madly in love with him.

Yep, he was a handsome devil all right.

"Picture him naked," Leigh Barrett whispered to Megan.

Stunned, Megan turned to stare at Chase's younger sister. "Excuse me?"

Thankfully, Leigh nodded toward the front of the room instead of in her brother's direction. "The mayor. When you're giving your presentation, if you get nervous, picture him naked."

Megan slipped her glasses down her nose and studied Earl Guthrie, the seventy-three-year-old mayor of Honey. When Earl caught her gaze, he gave Megan a benign, vague smile.

"I don't think so," Megan said to Leigh. "I prefer to think of Earl as fully clothed."

Leigh giggled. "Okay, maybe that wasn't such a hot idea after all. Let me see if I can find someone else for you to think of naked."

"That's not necessary. I'm not nervous." Megan flipped through her index cards.

Her argument was flawless, her plan foolproof. She had nothing to be nervous about. Besides, as the head librarian of the Honey Library, she knew every person in the room. This presentation would be a snap.

But with puppy-like enthusiasm, Leigh had already stood and was looking around. She hadn't spotted her oldest brother yet, but Megan knew it was only a matter of time before she did.

"Leigh, I'm fine," Megan tried, but Leigh finally saw Chase and yelled at him to come over and join them.

Chase made his way through the crowded room. The city council meetings usually drew a big audience, but Megan was happy to see even more people than usual had turned out to listen to her presentation of fundraiser ideas for new playground equipment.

When Chase got even with Megan and Leigh, he leaned across Megan to ruffle his sister's dark hair. Then he dropped into the folding chair next to Megan and winked at her. "Ladies, how are you tonight?"

Megan tried to keep her expression pleasant, but it wasn't easy. Ever since she'd moved back to Honey last year, pretending her feelings for Chase were platonic was proving harder and harder. At six-two, with deep black hair and even deeper blue eyes, he made her heart race and her palms sweat.

"Don't ruffle my hair, bozo." Leigh huffed at Megan's right, smoothing her hair. "I'm in college. I'm too old to have my hair ruffled."

To Megan's left, Chase chuckled. "Squirt, you're never going to be too old for me to ruffle your hair. When you're eighty, I'm going to totter up to you and do it."

"You and what orderly?" Leigh teased. "And just for the record, I like Nathan and Trent much better than I like you."

"Oh, please." Megan rolled her eyes at that one. Leigh loved all of her brothers, but everyone knew Chase was her favorite. When she was home from college, she always stayed with Chase.

"I love you, too, squirt," Chase said, not rising to his sister's taunt. Instead, he nudged Megan. "You okay?"

"I told her to imagine the mayor naked if she got

nervous, but she doesn't want to do that," Leigh supplied.

"I can see why not," Chase said. "Earl's not exactly stud-muffin material."

"Oooh, I know what she should do." Leigh practically bounced in her chair. "Megan, if you get nervous, picture Chase naked."

Megan froze and willed herself to stay calm. The absolute last thing she wanted to think about was Chase naked. Okay, maybe she did want to think of him naked, but not right now. Not right before she had to speak in front of a large portion of the entire town.

"I don't think so," Megan muttered, shooting a glare at Leigh.

The younger woman knew how Megan felt about her brother, and this was simply one more not-so-subtle attempt to get the two of them together. In the past few months, Leigh's matchmaking maneuvers had grown more extreme.

"I don't think I'll need to picture anyone naked," Megan stated.

On her other side, Chase offered, "Well, if you get flustered and it will make things easier for you, you go ahead and think of me naked, Megan. Whatever I can do to help."

Megan knew Chase was teasing her, but suddenly she realized how many years she'd wasted waiting for him to take her seriously.

She'd fallen for him when she'd moved to town at eight. Dreamed about him since she'd turned sixteen. And tried like the dickens to forget him when she'd been away at college and then later working at a library in Dallas for five years.

But nothing had helped. Not even seriously dating a man in Dallas had helped. In her soul, Megan believed she and Chase were meant to be together.

If only she could get him to notice her.

"Hey there, Chase," a smooth, feline voice fairly purred over their shoulders. "You're looking yummy. Like an especially luscious dessert, and I positively love dessert."

Oh, great. Megan glanced behind her. Janet Defries. Just what she needed tonight.

Chase smiled at the woman half leaning on his chair. "Hey, Janet. Do you plan on helping Megan with her committee?"

From the look on Janet's face, the only thing she planned on helping herself to was Chase, served on a platter.

She leaned toward Chase, the position no doubt deliberate since a generous amount of cleavage was exposed. "Are you going to help with this committee, Chase? Because if you are, I might be able to pry free a few hours."

Yeah, right. Megan shared a glance with Leigh. They both knew Janet would no more help with the committee than dogs would sing.

"I'd like to help, but it's a busy time on the ranch," Chase said.

"Shame." Janet slipped into the chair directly behind him. "I think you and I should figure out a way to spend some quality time together."

Her message couldn't have been clearer if she'd plastered it on a billboard. Megan hated herself for wanting to know, but she couldn't not look. She turned to see what Chase's reaction was to the woman's blatant come-on.

Mild interest. Megan repressed a sigh. Of course. Janet was exactly the type of woman Chase favored. One with a high-octane body and zero interest in a lasting relationship.

"Maybe we'll figure it out one of these days," Chase said, and Megan felt her temperature climb.

Okay, so she didn't have a drawer at home full of D-cups, but Megan knew she could make Chase happy. She could make him believe in love again.

If the dimwit would give her the chance.

Janet placed one hand on Chase's arm and licked her lips. "Well, you hurry up, else I might decide to go after Nathan or Trent instead. You're not the only handsome fella in your family."

Chase chuckled as he faced forward in his chair once again. "I sure am being threatened with my brothers tonight. But I'd like to point out that neither of them stopped by to lend their support, and I'm sitting here like an angel."

Leigh snorted. "Angel? You? Give me a break. You could make the devil himself blush, Chase Barrett."

Chase's grin was pure male satisfaction. "I do my best."

As Megan knew only too well. She'd watched him beguile a large percentage of the females in this part of Texas. Why couldn't he throw a little of that wickedness her way? Just once, she'd like to show him how combustible they could be together.

But even though she'd been back in Honey for almost a year, the man still treated her like a teenager. She'd just celebrated her twenty-ninth birthday. She wasn't a sheltered virgin with fairy-tale dreams of romance. She was a flesh and blood woman who knew what she wanted out of life.

She wanted Chase.

After a great deal of commotion getting the microphone to the right level, the mayor finally started the meeting. Within a few minutes, it was time for her presentation. Megan stood, adjusting her glasses.

"Remember, picture Chase naked if you get nervous," Leigh whispered but not very softly.

Megan was in the process of scooting past Chase, who had stood to let her by. She froze, standing directly in front of the man who consumed her dreams and starred in her fantasies.

He grinned.

"You know, I think I just may do that," Megan said. "And if he gets nervous, he can picture me naked, too."

❧

Had to be the heat, Chase decided as he settled back in the wobbly folding chair. Or maybe the water. Either way, something was weird because Megan Kendall had just flirted with him.

Leigh moved over to sit in the chair next to Chase. "You talk to Nathan or Trent today?"

Chase glanced at Megan, who was straightening her notes, so he had a couple of seconds to answer his sister. "Nathan and all of his employees are working overtime trying to get that computer program done. Trent has a new officer who joined the force today, so he's busy, too. You're stuck with me."

Rather than looking upset, Leigh's expression was downright blissful. "Megan and I are thrilled you're here."

Through narrowed eyes, Chase studied his sister. She was up to something as sure as the sun rose in the east, and he'd bet his prize bull it had something to do with him breaking up her necking session with Billy Joe Tate last night.

"Whatever you're doing, stop it," Chase told her. "It won't work."

Leigh fluttered her eyelashes at him, feigning innocence. "Who, me? I'm not up to anything. How could I be with you and Nathan and Trent on me every second of every day? I'm almost twenty-two, Chase."

"Spare me the melodrama. Just because I don't want my baby sister having wild sex in a classic Trans Am in front of my house doesn't make me a meddler."

Leigh snorted loud enough to make some of the ladies in the row in front of them turn to see what was happening. But Leigh, as usual, ignored everyone around her and barreled on.

"If it were up to my brothers, I'd still be a virgin," she actually hissed at him. "Thank goodness I decided to go away for college. No one in Austin has ever heard of the Barrett brothers."

Chase opened his mouth to say something but ended up gaping at his sister like a dead fish. He was still formulating what to say to Leigh's pronouncement when Megan started her presentation.

Good manners, drilled into him over the years, forced him to remain silent and listen to the speaker. But what in the blue bejesus was up with the women tonight? And why was he the lucky man who got to be trapped in the middle of it?

And since when wasn't Leigh a virgin? He glanced at his sister, who was nodding and smiling at Megan as she went over the reasons why the city park needed new playground equipment.

He had to face facts. Their father had run off with a waitress when Leigh had been four. Their mother had died when Leigh had been eleven. She'd been raised by three older brothers who might have been strict with her but who did a fair amount of hell-raising on their own.

He should count his lucky stars that Leigh hadn't made him an uncle already.

But for crying out loud. He was all for liberated women, but did they all have to liberate themselves in front of him at the same time?

He turned away from Leigh, but not before making a mental note to talk to her once more about safe sex and nice boys.

Behind him, Chase could actually feel Janet Defries staring at the back of his head. No doubt she was planning all the things she could do to him if she had plastic wrap and an economy jar of mayonnaise.

And then there was Megan. Frowning, he looked at her. She was carefully explaining how the city could build a large play castle like so many bigger cities had if they raised enough money and had enough volunteers.

Her talk was going well, as expected, but Chase

could tell she was nervous. They'd been friends for so long, he recognized the signs.

He gave her an encouraging smile.

And the look she gave back scorched him. Good Lord. She was picturing him naked.

Before he could stop himself, before he could even think about how downright stupid it was, he found himself picturing Megan naked, too.

And really, really liking what he pictured. Sure, a few times over the years, he'd turned the idea of Megan over in his mind. After all, she was attractive in a sedate sort of way.

She had long ash-blond hair, pretty green eyes, and a slim body with just enough curves to keep a man interested. Sweet curves that would be soft to the touch, and silky to the taste and—

Whoa. What in the blazes was he doing? Megan Kendall was one of his best friends, not to mention a woman who actually believed in things like love and marriage. He blinked and mentally tossed a thick, woolen blanket over Megan's naked body. That would be the end of that.

"I think Chase should co-chair the committee with Megan," Leigh announced, bringing Chase's attention back to the meeting going on around him.

He glared at Leigh. "What? I don't have time to co-chair a committee." He glanced at the city council, the mayor, and finally, at Megan. "Sorry. I'm too busy at the moment."

"Everyone is busy," Earl said. "But you make time for something as important as this." The mayor leaned forward. "Don't you want your children to have a nice park to play in someday, Chase?"

"I don't have any children, Earl, and I don't plan on having any."

He looked at Megan, whose expression could only be called sad. Great. Just great. Now he'd disappointed her by saying he wouldn't co-chair the committee. Well, at least he'd found a way to get her to stop picturing him naked.

"Hold on a minute here," Leigh said. "It's your turn to help, Chase Barrett. Trent's the chief of police, so he does a lot for this town. And Nathan's computer company supports practically everybody. I've volunteered at the senior center, and I'm coming back to town next fall to do my student teaching. It's your turn to do something to help."

A slow, steady throbbing sensation started somewhere in the back of Chase's brain. Leave it to his sister to put him in an awkward position. "I don't have the time right now, Leigh. I'll be happy to make a donation, though."

Megan's expression softened. She forgave him. He knew she forgave him. Naturally, sweet Megan would understand.

Dang it. Now he felt lower than a rattlesnake's rump.

"What would it involve?" he half groaned, wanting to do whatever it took to get out of this room and away from these women.

"It wouldn't be much," Megan told him. "Just help with the carnival and the auction. I'd only need a couple hours of your time for the next few weeks."

Like he believed that. A carnival and an auction sounded like a lot of work. "Why do we have to have both?"

Leigh thwacked him on the arm. "Weren't you listening? Megan explained that the carnival will bring in the people, then the auction will bring in the big money."

Chase frowned at his sister. "Oh."

"I'll be willing to help on this committee if Chase is co-chair," Janet said from over his shoulder.

The throbbing in the back of his head grew more intense as several other single women in the room also agreed to help on the committee, that is of course, "if he did, too."

"See there, Chase, you're a popular guy. Lots of folks want to help out if you join in," Earl said. He glanced at the members of the city council. "I think this sounds like a great plan. Let's take a vote."

Chase wasn't surprised the council agreed with the mayor. What wasn't to like? Everyone was happy except for him.

"I never agreed to help," he pointed out to Leigh after Megan gathered her things and headed back to sit down.

"Oh, let it go, Chase. You're like a neutered hound dog, going on about something that's long gone," Leigh said.

A soft, sexy, feminine laugh floated around him, raising his body temperature. Who in the world... He turned, bumping right into Megan. The smile she gave him was so very unlike the Megan he'd known for years and years.

Her smile was pure seduction.

"Trust me, Chase is nothing like a neutered hound dog," she said softly.

The water. Something was definitely wrong with the water in this town.

Don't miss the first book in the Handsome Devils series. Order now.

ABOUT THE AUTHORS

Liz Alvin

Liz Alvin has loved reading and writing for as long as she can remember. In fact, she majored in literature at college just so she could spend her days reading great stories. When it came to her own stories, she decided to write romances with happy endings because she's a firm believer in love. She's been married to her own hero for over 30 years. They live in Texas near their adult children and are surrounded by rescue dogs and a rescue cat.

Lori Wilde

Lori Wilde is the New York Times, USA Today and Publishers' Weekly bestselling author of 88 works of romantic fiction. She's a three time Romance Writers' of America RITA finalist and has four times been nominated for Romantic Times Readers' Choice Award. She has won numerous other awards as well.

Her books have been translated into 26 languages, with more than four million copies of her books sold worldwide.

Her breakout novel, *The First Love Cookie Club*, has been optioned for a TV movie.

Lori is a registered nurse with a BSN from Texas

Christian University. She holds a certificate in forensics, and is also a certified yoga instructor.

A fifth generation Texan, Lori lives with her husband, Bill, in the Cutting Horse Capital of the World; where they run Epiphany Orchards, a writing/creativity retreat for the care and enrichment of the artistic soul.

Made in the USA
Monee, IL
23 January 2020